PLAYING OUT OF THE DEEP WOODS

PLAYING OUT OF THE DEEP WOODS

Stories by G. W. Hawkes

UNIVERSITY OF MISSOURI PRESS
COLUMBIA AND LONDON

Copyright © 1995 by G. W. Hawkes
University of Missouri Press, Columbia, Missouri 65201
Printed and bound in the United States of America
All rights reserved
5 4 3 2 1   99 98 97 96 95

Library of Congress Cataloging-in-Publication Data

Hawkes, G. W., 1953–
    Playing out of the deep woods : stories / by G. W. Hawkes.
        p.   cm.
    ISBN 0-8262-0988-2 (alk. paper)
    I. Title.
PS3558.A818P57 1995
813'.54—dc20   94-36965
                                                          CIP

⊚™ This paper meets the requirements of the
American National Standard for Permanence of Paper
for Printed Library Materials, Z39.48, 1984.

Designer: Kristie Lee
Typesetter: Connell-Zeko Type & Graphics
Printer and binder: Thomson-Shore, Inc.
Typefaces: Caslon 224 and Copperplate 33bc

For acknowledgments, see page 141.

FOR MY TEACHERS

John Gardner, Charles Johnson,

Barry Targan, John Vernon,

Larry Woiwode

CONTENTS

The Foundation   1

Always Cold   18

The Movable Hazard   32

Peeper   42

Gardener   53

The Last American Living in Cuba   59

Playing Out of the Deep Woods   65

The Practice Court-Martial of Private Peterson   77

Mutiny   91

Stupid-Proof   103

The Shortest Hole   115

Corpus Christi   123

Pull, Ponies, Pull, My Dearhearts   131

PLAYING OUT OF THE DEEP WOODS

THE FOUNDATION

An institute of this size should have on its thick letterhead a masculine city like *Boston* or *Chicago* (or even *Los Angeles*), but The Foundation rises from the level plain like a dirty ice cube in Mott, North Dakota. One can stand on any street corner and watch the sky of the apocalypse skid across its three stories of smoked glass; at night the city's traffic lights blink back like eyes.

Tharp had been living in a tent out in the shale hills of Montana for nearly two years, his only company the last six months a bright, talkative tribe of meadowlarks and a prospector with a plate in his head who thought the year was 1946, but even so, Mott looked small. The sky had all the colors of ripe peaches, swirling like syrup in The Foundation's reflection. He watched gloomily as the bus growled off to other exotic places. *Bismarck,* and *Fargo.*

The letter said he should report *immediately you arrive,* so he hefted the valise he carries when he wants to appear academic, even though all he had in it was his notebook and a change of clothes, walked past a hotel and a shower and a meal, and knocked on the black, mirrored glass with the misspent faith that somebody was inside.

Apparently, nobody was.

He knocked a second time, and then a third, and then cupped his hands around his eyes and tried to see in. All he got was a close look at his own dark eye.

"Well . . . *damn* it."

They'd hurried him back from the field with a letter, and

he'd hurried to come. For nineteen months he'd netted mead-owlarks (no easy trick), imprisoned them, weighed them and measured them, drawn their blood and shipped the labeled vials to North Dakota (he should be able to fix watches after this, or work the tiny clasps on necklaces), and then set the birds loose again. Who wouldn't hurry to be done with that?

The year before, he'd finished his bachelor's degree in zo-ology and taken the scholarship they'd offered. (He suspected he'd been chosen on the strength of a paper he'd cribbed from his roommate.) If he'd known the loneliness and the labor that was waiting he would have refused all of it—the money and the promise of a career—and gone back to busing tables.

Now this.

The letter mentioned a new assignment. He was eager to know it. The Foundation could send him anywhere to do anything—anywhere at all, so long as they didn't ask him to siphon blood from songbirds—and he would go happily. Send me to Afghanistan to collect rocks, he thought. Send me to New Guinea to count spiders.

Let me inside. The building took up a city block. He'd make one circuit, he decided, and then give up and find a hotel.

Each side was the same. It was as if he'd never left the place he'd started from: the same wall of glass looked back at him, the same double door was set in the center, the same square pavement blocks unfolded in a checkerboard under his feet. A momentary panic was hurried along by a white lab coat disappearing into the dark building.

"Wait!"

The coat paused, half obscured by the door; a hand at the end of a cuff beckoned, and he ran.

The hand belonged to a Chinese who stood about six-six. It had square, clean, long nails and a ring with a black stone on the little finger. It held the door open and then slipped into the pocket of the lab coat.

"You're Tharp," the man said.

Tharp nodded.

"We've been expecting you."

"The bus," Tharp said, waving vaguely.

"I know. This way."

The building's interior was a series of rectangular, upright volumes of space separated by cellophane sculptures that drifted the whole long way down from the third-floor ceiling. Soft green lights made them look like translucent stones. These almost-empty areas enclosed a small, vertical core of offices. The Chinese scientist led him to the nearest stairwell.

"Down," he said.

"Down?"

"We're an iceberg. The laboratories are downstairs. The storage areas. The map. All the real work goes on underneath."

"The map?"

The head in front of Tharp nodded, but that might have been because it was wobbling on the top of a tall, white pole already making the first turn half a flight away, racing down the stairs.

It was the map, in the weeks to come, that pulled at Tharp like a vague but exciting guilt, interrupting a conversation or a meal, keeping him awake and troubling his dreams by turns. It was the map, and the huge vault built to hold it, that was the center of The Foundation's vast basement, the heart of the maze, and seemingly the underpinning of Mott itself.

The Chinese, a man known to all as Dr. X, had paraded him past a dozen other scientists whose names were now a blur, given him a room—"We keep guest quarters here as well," he had been told—but no assignments, and no instructions. He'd wanted to ask, but some small gesture of grace had stopped him in time. He had soon found that he was free to roam about the place, and in less than a week he was opening doors and peering inside with the nonchalant curiosity of someone visiting the house he'd grown up in.

What work went on here he still didn't know, but he was beginning to suspect it would be easier to find out what research didn't. Agronomy? Oceanography? Aeronautics? The place had hydroponic gardens, huge tanks of bubbling, murky seawater, and in one room on a flat, dark, plastic slab lay something looking suspiciously like a missile.

Dr. X was right: The Foundation spread out in all directions underneath, as if that space were needed to provide massive structural support for those fluted columns of green air above.

Tharp, when he could, made himself useful. He did this because counting rocks in Afghanistan or spiders in New Guinea no longer seemed such a prize and because always haunting him was the prospect of drawing blood from still another bird population. He'd put on a lab coat at any hour and wander into laboratories, holding a thingamajig or twiddling a doodad or sending juice into a whatchamacallit at somebody's nod. When he wasn't needed, he'd slip into the maproom and stare at the map.

It was a textured hologram whose controls he hadn't yet discovered (and wasn't sure he'd have the courage to use once he did; he wouldn't fiddle with a Van Gogh just because somebody put one into his hands). For the time being, he was content to watch whatever display was up.

Up, once, in that dark room was the blue Earth, circled by its dead-yellow, clay-colored moon and another, lumpy, larger one; in the far reaches of the vault a red planet hovered that Tharp thought must be the desert of Mars. But as he watched, the second moon spun away in a long loop and glanced off the planet, and Tharp ducked as the room filled with intangible shards. Like an imaginary kaleidoscope exploding, he thought.

This time, two men stood like gods over wrinkled mountains and pink flatlands. The map was bisected with a thin, fluorescent-green line he'd come to recognize as state borders: Colorado and New Mexico. The map receded until he could see the jigsaw-puzzle right-angled panhandles of Oklahoma and Texas. A small blue triangle appeared where the states collided.

"See? Right there," a voice said. "Now, watch."

New Mexico and its mountains rushed up and Tharp, still unused to the map, recoiled.

"Here, in the Sangre de Cristos."

Blue triangles appeared like thrown stars, a tiny spiral in the mountains.

"Maybe."

"Maybe, hell. *Here* and *here* and *here* and *here*." Each blue light glowed in turn.

"That's still those two out there, isn't it? What are their names?"

"Suope and Merline, yes. And a new man, Peters."

"Jesus, they've been there their whole lives."

A shudder ran through Tharp. It could have been him, alone with the meadowlarks.

"So, what do you think?"

"You know the rules as well as I do: you need a minimum of seven for a pattern. Four is only a second-level coincidence."

The other one jabbed a thumb at Tharp. "Ask him, then."

"What's he been doing?"

"Birds. In Montana, or someplace."

"In Montana," Tharp agreed.

They turned on him. "What do you see?"

Tharp stepped closer. "It depends on what the blue triangles represent," he said.

"Don't tell him."

Don't tell him? Oh, Jesus God, he hated exams. He was convinced that this was one and that if he failed it he'd be back in the field, a blue triangle—or whatever—on this map.

Tharp studied it helplessly, as if in his own nightmare: a text he hadn't read; a text he didn't know how to read. Seeing nothing would be easiest but not altogether true. Which of the two scientists should he agree with (which of them, that is, had the power to send him back to Montana)?

"Enlarge it, please," he said.

One of the men touched a button on a remote control, channel hopping, and the triangles leaped at him. The mountains appeared so huge that Tharp felt he could hide in their folds.

"The other way," he said. "Smaller, I guess it would be."

Texas panhandle. Oklahoma panhandle. Another blue triangle.

"Again, please."

"How small do you want to go?"

Tharp shrugged.

The map jumped again, the green lines of borders now countries, curving with the Earth.

"Can you make the triangles bigger, or brighter, or something?"

"Hell, yes."

One in Mexico, two in Hawaii, one in Seattle, and a spray of them across the heart of Canada.

"Smaller," Tharp said, meaning the map. "Bigger," he said, meaning the triangles, but the man was already busy with the controls, and in a moment the globe rotated in front of them, the triangles now lasers of blue light. The maproom looked like a disco.

"I'll be damned," the other one said.

The comma started in the Sangre de Cristos and spiraled outward in a shape all schoolchildren knew. "Get a star map," Tharp said, but the others were already nodding.

They all seemed to know his name now. Some even stuck a *Dr.* in front of it, out of good humor, he supposed. They nodded or waved when they passed him in the labyrinth of passageways. And The Director invited him to lunch.

Tharp went to see Dr. X.

"Lunch, huh?"

"What do I do?"

"Eat."

"I mean, what do I say to him?"

"That depends on what he wants to talk about," Dr. X said, and then took pity on Tharp. "Look, he's not as bad as everybody says."

"Does everybody say that?"

"You haven't heard the rumors? I thought that was why you'd come."

Tharp shook his head, genuinely worried now.

"To start with, he lives upstairs," Dr. X said. "That makes a lot of these folks nervous. Usually, you don't go to see him unless you're being fired. Or sent someplace . . . difficult."

"Difficult?"

"Dangerous."

"Maybe he just wants to pat me on the head," Tharp said, "and tell me I was a good boy."

"Maybe."

"You don't think so?"

Dr. X shrugged. "It's happened before, once or twice, or so I've heard. You can't ever tell with Arlyle. Go. Eat. Listen. Learn."

"What are those damned blue triangles?"

Dr. X smiled.

"Nobody will tell me."

"Me, either," Dr. X said.

Tharp was ready for lunch an hour early, as uncomfortable in the new white shirt and narrow black tie he'd bought in town as if he were going on a date. He hadn't the money with him to replace his ragged blue jeans or tennis shoes. He'd hoped the creases would fall out of the shirt, but they hadn't yet.

He climbed up to the third floor and stood outside Arlyle's office, looked at his watch, and then took the stairs back down to the lobby and stood around down there. He looked at his watch again. Then he went outside and stood there. He felt as if he were in high school again, waiting to take Elizabeth to the movies.

The thing to do, he thought to himself, was to say as little as possible and eat without splashing any of it on The Director. Try to look intelligent. Try to look valuable. More than anything, try not to look like somebody who could be sent back out into the wilds to take blood samples from birds.

He sucked in the spring air of North Dakota (much as he had once sucked in the spring air of Connecticut), hitched his jeans up with his thumbs, and climbed up to the third floor for lunch.

"So," Arlyle said, shaking his hand, "how did you get along with the meadowlarks?"

Christ. "Just fine," he said.

"Oh?"

What does he want from me? he wondered. What was it about this place—and everybody in it—that kept you guessing? "Fine," he said again. "Just fine." And then he blushed at his stupid lies and looked down at his sneakers.

Arlyle looked down at them too. He was tall and bald and impeccably dressed, and he held his glasses in one hand away from his body as if he didn't know where to put them. His own shoes were oxblood beneath a painful shine.

"Well," he said, and shrugged, and smiled. "Good, good."

I've done it, Tharp thought. I've just got myself sent back into the field.

"I want you to go someplace for me," Arlyle said, as if Tharp had spoken aloud. "For The Foundation. I hear you've been very helpful. But first, let's have something to eat."

"Go where?" Tharp blurted out.

Arlyle smiled again at him. "You're eager, yes? Still, it's only to be expected, I suppose; this dark, stuffy building is no place for a young man. Only old people about."

"Yes, it is."

"Nonsense. Here, eat."

Tharp looked at the plates of thin sandwiches that had been brought in. "I don't want to eat, Dr. Arlyle. And I don't want to go back"—he waved a hand—"out there."

"But that's what we do, son." Arlyle mimicked his wave. "We work *out there.*"

"If I see another meadowlark," Tharp said, "I'll throw up."

"This isn't meadowlarks."

"I hate Montana."

"This isn't Montana."

"I want to work with the map."

"You will, you will." Arlyle took Tharp by an elbow and steered him to the sandwiches. "I think you're right for analysis; in fact, I have no doubts about it. You've impressed Bernard, and that isn't often done. But first—after you eat, of course—you have to go someplace."

I won't do it, Tharp thought, but what he said was, "Where?"

"Kauai," Arlyle said. "In Hawaii."

"Why?"

"To look for more little blue triangles," Arlyle said. He smiled a third time. "That's what you want, isn't it?"

He handed Tharp a sandwich, and Tharp thought that if he refused it Arlyle would put it in his mouth for him. "Our man in the islands is pulling up the—what should we call them? figurines?—by the bushel basket." Arlyle's hand closed over his. "We want to have a look at them, and Bernard won't hear of sending anybody but you."

Tharp didn't know anything about Hawaii, but he thought if he decided to quit The Foundation it would be a good place from which to turn in his resignation.

During the long flight from San Francisco he'd looked down at the black Pacific and thought of Bernard's glowing triangles, or, more accurately, of the things those triangles represented: the tiny figures in wood or clay or stone that kept popping up. We'll find them on the sea bottom, too, dropped overboard by early seafarers.

He shook his head. They must be scattered thick as the dust in an old house, arranged in the layers of the planet in long, spiraling arms.

He arrived in Hawaii with the sun, landing at dawn in Honolulu. Standing on the tarmac, gripping his valise, he was overwhelmed by the gentleness of the air, the perfect temperature, and the scent of flowers. Young women were everywhere. A bird called. Tharp didn't flinch.

His connecting flight to Kauai was met by one of The Foundation's oldest operatives, a professor emeritus of Polynesian cultures and—reputedly—a thoroughly irascible old man.

"You Tharp?"

Tharp nodded.

"Then get in." He pointed to an old yellow Subaru station wagon. "Where'd you do your work?"

"Montana."

The man made a noise that sounded like a fart. "You're an expert in these things, and you did your work in *Montana*?" He ground the Subaru's first gear.

"I'm an expert in meadowlarks," Tharp said. "Montana's full to the brim with meadowlarks."

"None in Hawaii," he said. Second gear sounded as if it were being sheared. "Who sent you?"

"Arlyle."

"Why?"

"I haven't a clue."

Third gear howled. "I always suspected they didn't know what they were doing," he said. "But up till now it didn't matter 'cause they've left me alone."

Tharp nodded apologetically.

"You don't know anything about art?"

Tharp shook his head. "Bird blood."

The old professor's eyebrows rose, as if this could (somehow) be useful after all. "What do you know about it?"

"How to get it out of the bird without it killing him," Tharp said.

"Who cares?"

"Exactly," Tharp said.

They drove a while without speaking after that.

Tharp hadn't known the world could be this green. The jungle was so vibrant that the cream of the ocean seemed to have picked up its colors. The thunderheads building over the Pacific looked like blocks of old ice. The knife-edged mountains, crawling with life, tumbled into the sea. Everywhere there was the noise of birds and the cloying smell of flowers.

"You're one of the new kind, aren't you?" the old professor said. He still hadn't introduced himself.

"How's that?" Tharp asked.

The old man waved a hand, looking for a word. "Accountants," he said, making a face as if the word itself were bitter, "only interested in tables and columns. That's it, isn't it?"

"No," Tharp said. "I'm interested—and I just found this out—in patterns."

"Same thing."

"No, it's not. The only figures I'm interested in right now are the ones in bikinis, and all I care about your figurines are that they've turned up in other places as well."

The old professor shrugged. "Why shouldn't they? They're made with human hands," he said, "from the human figure. What else would you expect?"

"I don't know."

"They're male, is all."

"They are?"

"Jesus, haven't you seen one?"

Tharp shook his head. "The Foundation's going to call them in. From all over."

"Then why not stay there and wait for them?"

"I don't know," he said again. "They wanted me to come out here and see what you've found." He looked out the window at the hills. "Maybe they thought you wouldn't send them yours." Or maybe Hawaii was meant as a vacation, a reward.

"Damn right I won't send mine."

Then that's it, Tharp thought. The first thing.

"Why should I?"

"Look," Tharp said, "I don't know how anything works; I'm the new kid around here. I just got off the bus. That building in North Dakota is the spookiest place you ever want to see— all basement—full of spooky scientists—people a lot like you—and nobody tells anybody anything. That seems to be the rule. They dragged me in from Montana—thank God— away from those damned birds, but never did tell me why. It's an accident that I'm here and I sometimes think the whole freaking Foundation runs on that principle. That, and keeping us away from civilians. And each other.

"What I've gathered is this: The Foundation is the sole support, or at the least a good second paycheck, for a lot of people in white coats busily at work in their own little corners of the world doing exactly what they want to do, people who otherwise—without the help of The Foundation—wouldn't be able to. Those lifetimes of labor are sent back to Mott, North Dakota, in rotting cardboard boxes and crates of old bones and reams of reports and statistics, and they are funneled into a room they have that is sort of a magical map, and every once in a while somebody discovers a connection between whatever it is that is going on in China and whatever it is that is going on in Borneo, and maybe that's all The Foundation ever wanted in the first place.

"So cranky old bastards like you can live here in Hawaii and complain and have things your own way and also cash the checks they send once a month and still go on with your life's work, and somebody like me can show up—and not even know why, exactly—and you can give him hell and make his life miserable."

Tharp paused for a needed breath. "That's why."

They drove on for a few minutes, the old professor frowning into his mirror. "You almost make it all sound admirable," he said.

"It's not," Tharp said. "I hate it."

"Maybe you just hate me."

"That, too."

The old man pulled the Subaru off to the side and then spun in the gravel around in a U-turn.

Back to the airport, Tharp thought.

"Name's Frank," he said, over the sound of another grinding gear.

Tharp considered that, and what to do next. "Steven," he finally said. "Steve. Where are we going now?"

"My place, to show you those figurines."

"Where *were* we going?"

"Out to one of the sites. Where you would have seen diddly-squat."

His house looked like an accumulation of odd parts clinging without any apparent help to a hillside. The roof was corrugated tin. A wooden deck jutting out from the second floor reached out over the tops of flowering trees. The windows were frosted slats of glass set in louvers without screens. Inside, the bare floors and simple furniture and the books neatly arranged in tall bookshelves all looked scrubbed.

"Drink?"

"That's the first anyone's asked in the nearly two years I've worked for this outfit."

"Fine. Drink?"

"Yes, please."

Frank sighed. *"Drink?"*

"Oh. Beer."

"Good. Sit down somewhere."

Tharp sat carefully. "Make this yourself?"

"Make what?" Frank called from the kitchen.

"This chair."

"Which one are you sitting in?"

Tharp described it.

"Made all of them," Frank said.

"Jesus, you're exasperating."

"Yes." Frank brought two beers. "It's probably not possible to study something without wanting to make it yourself. I'm an expert on carvings. So I carve furniture out of logs. I carve, and you . . ."

"That's a stumper," Tharp said.

"Not really."

"Technically," Tharp said, "I'm a vampire."

"That's Arlyle's position. You're a transfusion. Every organization needs one once every decade or so."

"Arlyle's not going to give me his job."

"You wouldn't want it. All I meant was you're better than you think at drawing blood."

"That's not a transfusion."

"It's the first part of one. Christ, you're harder to get along with than I am. Now, look here," he said, and began pulling little carved statues out from odd corners of the room.

He lined a dozen of them up on the coffee table. They were the size of fingers, blatantly male and rigidly erect.

Tharp picked one up and it struck him that he was holding right angles.

"Some others have got some like these out of Africa," Frank said, "but not too many other places. It's rare, oddly, to see something like this. Fertility figures are usually female." He cupped his hands so they faced each other. "Large hips. Large breasts."

"I've seen pictures."

"I'll bet," he said dryly. "Anyway, the small size of these is interesting, considering their phallic nature. And the tiny hole bored through just there, at the neck. The wood is koa, a favorite of local craftsmen, because it's soft, easy to work."

"A charm," Tharp said.

"Very good. A charm. These were worn, probably around the neck. By men or women, I can't say."

"Women," Tharp said.

"How do you know?"

Tharp shrugged. "I don't. Yet."

Frank smiled. "Maybe you've just got women on your mind. I'm sure you'll let me know when you find out. It'll sure bollix things up." He sat back and drank his beer, all the while staring at Tharp.

Those eyes, magnified by spectacles and reflecting the beer can's aluminum rim, made Tharp nervous. They were, he reminded himself, an examiner's eyes.

"What do you want from me?" he asked.

"Nothing, why?"

"You're plotting something."

"You've spent too long by yourself, kid. An old man like me has left all his plotting days behind him."

"Why do you think these are fertility figures?" Tharp asked.

"What else would they be?"

Tharp shrugged. "This isn't my line of country."

"If that"—Frank pointed—"isn't potency, I don't know what is."

Tharp shrugged again. "Maybe they're badges of rank, or they ward off evil spirits, or something. Maybe they're a primitive sort of pornography."

"We call those aphrodisiacs."

"Whatever. We can't guess, yet. Maybe we can guess when we have them all, when we know where they've come from. Do you know that they're turning up in a large spiral that circles the globe? Bernard's excited about that."

"Bernard?"

"One of the scientists back in Mott."

"Bernard's his last name?"

"I don't know."

"I wonder if it's the Bernard who wrote a paper twenty years ago on the sex life of the spiny lobster."

Tharp thought about it. "I don't think so, but again, I don't know."

"I hope not," Frank said. "That man was an idiot."

Tharp turned it over and over in his hands and asked for another beer. "Women ever make any art?" he asked finally.

It was Frank's turn to shrug. "I guess they must have. Art spans quite a gap. What are you getting at?"

"Well, I'm thinking of the cave paintings, now, the only early art I've ever studied. We think of the artist as the hunter, don't we, but what if she was the cook?"

"What if that cave art isn't anything more than a shopping list?"

"Exactly. And it was, either way. Isn't the theory that art was a sort of sympathetic magic: you know, draw a likeness first of the beast you want to capture?"

"Then what's this?" Frank picked up one of the figurines.

"Art by the women, a likeness of what they wanted to capture?"

Tharp laughed. "Why not that?"

"You'll have a hell of a time convincing most people that women were ever artists."

"I'm not out to convince anybody of anything. But I'd say if men did these, it's ego. Bragging. Silly big peacocks without feathers. There's nothing new about that. What I hated most about those meadowlarks was their damned singing, from morning until after dark, day after day for nearly two years. The males busted a gut—or a gizzard, or whatever—to outsing the other males and attract a mate."

"And your point?"

Tharp looked into his beer, hoping to find an answer. What was his point? "Maybe," he said slowly, "that if men made these, then we've gotten worse, or at least no better. That we've never been anything but a bunch of self-serving bastards. Maybe it's true, I don't know: a lot of posturing still goes on—and always has; God knows I feel like going down to the beach and doing some of it myself—but isn't this stuff"— he turned the figurine around so it faced Frank—"art, I guess—about something else entirely?" Tharp waved a hand that took in the room. "Your furniture. You said we make the things we love. Envision it first. Reproduce it. Capture it."

Frank studied him for a moment, and Tharp felt studied. "It's as good a definition as I know," Frank said. "Now go sell it to the rest of the world."

He had two of the tiny figures with him on the plane, packed in wood shavings in their own little handcrafted caskets. When he got the other ones from the field—from New Mexico and the Yucatan and the Northwest and Canada (and the ones from Africa and Australia and who knew where else)—he'd see what there was to see.

His theory was probably nonsense, but that was okay. He didn't want to sell the world on anything. He hadn't invested any part of himself in it. It wasn't the sex of the figures or the figure-makers that held any interest for him; it was where those figures had been left behind to be found, the pattern that emerged in a globe too large for its inhabitants to comprehend.

He'd never understood in college why art isn't any more beautiful now than it was at the start, or how—according to his literature professors—we got poetry right the first time. It's because we have more than blood in us, he thought: the galaxy shape—that larger design—is built in. It had to be sympathetic magic. Draw the thing. Pull it closer.

He took one of the men out of his box and held it. His seatmate, a woman, gasped, and Tharp smiled.

He ran a finger down its tiny spine. The red, wide-grained koa was the color of fire, as soft as feathers, as warm as blood. Tharp felt something inside him flutter and rise. It rose like an exclamation—a dissimulation—an exaltation of larks.

Always Cold

Even though the flatness of Kansas is sometimes exaggerated, I'll admit it's level in places. It's particularly level around Oracle, so flat that, for a week at the equinoxes, the sunlight skips across town like a thrown rock. Women have to hold their skirts down to keep that light from jumping up. A wariness steals into their eyes, like when the man from the bank drives out, and they grip their handbags more tightly, and the men push their hands down into their trouser pockets in fists.

September (and, more rarely, March) is the time of Accidents. In Oracle at this time of year an ambivalence grips all of us, a bit like the expectation that must take hold of a wife who hears a car door and has a husband who drinks. The dark doesn't help; porch lights burn at noon for those six months, and the sky looks as if a fire is close. Even though this is only a trick of topography and light, we stare out our windows for a sign.

This last Accident began with Ruth Montgomery, a woman born and raised so close by that she grew up knowing that Septembers in Oracle are dangerous. She'd had the Hardwells out in August to fix her roof, put down new treads on the basement stairs, and clamp the loose rain pipe by the kitchen window, and after she'd paid them off she'd walked around with a wrench and a screwdriver and tightened everything that rattled. Then the weird light of September began skidding around, and the next morning she slipped in the middle of her living room as if that soft yellow pine were ice.

She didn't break anything, but she said she got headaches bad enough to make her blind. Ruth isn't one to complain, so it took her a week to come in to see the doctor. He prescribed aspirin and rest and said she should consider going down to Dodge City and having Memorial Hospital take a look at her brain. Ruth said that although she was relatively uninhibited and didn't need much privacy, she did need some, and she'd be damned if she'd let anybody look at that. She went home and suffered for another week. Finally, she called my mother, hoping for one of the remedies she's famous for, and my mother took me along when she visited Ruth, as my mother doesn't drive.

I used to cut the grass and such for Miss Montgomery— years ago, now—and I didn't mind at all going back after all this time to see if I could help.

"Help?" Ruth asked. "Lord, yes, boy," she said, and winked. "You can find a pickaxe and hammer it on that floor some. Rough it up so I don't fall again." She sat on the sofa and waved the two of us to chairs. She held a hand in front of her eyes as if the room were bright. "Or you can pour us a couple of fingers of bourbon all around. I'll have mine on ice with ginger ale."

Liquor cabinets in the Midwest are sometimes ingeniously hidden affairs, sliding out on tracks from under an appliance, or dropping from a false ceiling on pulleys, but Ruth—true to her nature—kept her store in a kitchen cabinet, next to the cereal.

She's always been a drinker. She'd splash a bit of bourbon into the bottom of a glass of warm milk after I'd raked leaves all Saturday, or in the winter she'd set the glass down in front of me before I started shoveling her walk, and she'd say— with a conspiratorial grin and a wink—"Let's see if that warms you up some." I never much liked the taste of milk with bourbon in it, so at sixteen or so I stopped drinking the stuff. I pulled the square bottle and three glasses down and filled them with ice and liquor, and topped two of the drinks with the wintry-colored ginger ale. When I got back, my mother and Ruth had their heads together and their hands on each other's knees, whispering in the way only women can.

"Let's see if that warms you up some," I said, and handed Ruth her whiskey.

She looked puzzled, then suspicious. "Did I tell you I was cold?"

"No, ma'am."

"Well, I am. Lately, I'm always cold." She cupped her hands around the cold glass as if she were drawing heat from it. "And I don't dream anymore."

"Do you think the two are connected?" my mother asked.

"I thought everybody dreamed," I said.

They both gave me looks.

"I don't know," she said to my mother. She took a good slug of her drink and I watched it travel.

My mother concentrated in the way she does when she's mentally writing things down. "What about the headaches?" she asked.

"They're terrible," Ruth said.

"Constant?"

Ruth shook her head slowly, as if she weren't certain, or as if she were being careful not to start a new one. "They come and go," she said. "I get sort of a hum all the time, now, like bees, then it gets louder, then it stops completely. Then the headache comes. God, Louise," she said to my mother, "it's like giving birth with your eyes."

I could see my mother, her hands still, jotting all this down in her head. "What else?"

"Just this coldness."

"You're cold now?"

"I'm freezing."

She wasn't; not to look at her. Outside it looked like dusk, of course, as it was the middle of the afternoon at the end of September. It sure wasn't shirtsleeve weather, but it was twenty degrees warmer in the house, and cozy, and Ruth had on a man's flannel blue-and-black-check work shirt and jeans, the cuffs rolled back on both of them.

"Teeth chatter?" my mother asked.

"No."

"Chills?"

"No. Only this—cold." She shook her head again, to prove she couldn't adequately explain it.

"Are you sleeping all right?"

"Except for the dreams—or lack of them. When the head-ache goes. Sometimes I have to sleep in the afternoons, or in the mornings, and it takes a good amount of this"—she raised her glass—"to put me out."

"You took a good knock on the head."

Ruth laughed, and looked younger and healthier. "I sure did. I went down like a kid on skates for the first time: flat out with my arms like a scarecrow's. Like falling back into a snowdrift. I knocked it good. It bounced twice."

"Got a bump?"

"Now that's the weird thing," Ruth said. "I never did. I felt for it a couple of times, figuring it would come up, and now I'm beginning to worry that the bump's on the inside."

My mother nodded as if that made sense. Ruth looked at me, a little surprised that I was still there, and then my mother turned in her chair to look at me too. My mother's look said I was excused.

"I'll be out back," I said, though why I wanted to stand outside in the growing dark I don't know.

Ruth's yard—like a great many yards in Oracle—is the edge of somebody's crop, separated from it by a couple of trees thrown up a half-century before. The yards bordered, now, on the ruin of the season: pumpkin-colored, in this light, the wheat stubble spread into the gloom like the after-math it was.

A wind freshened and dragged my thin hair across my eyes. I pushed it back to cover my bald spot. I remember thinking that we'd come all this way for not much reason, as Ruth looked well enough (and not crazy, as I'd feared), and there was certainly no inkling then of this being Oracle's annual Accident. I wished I'd brought the Jack Daniel's out with me, as the wind was beginning to cut and I was feeling the cold that Ruth must have blowing inside her.

House lots are wide on the edges of fields and, squinting, I could just make out her nearest neighbor—either Jack Farley or his wife (it was hard to know in that light)—standing bundled up and looking out at the end of the crop the way I was. I ambled in that direction the way a dog will in a neighborhood he's not certain of, willing to be friendly, willing to be run off.

It was Jack. He's older than me by half a dozen years, but at our age that's the same as growing up together. After forty, we all go along alike until we get old.

"Will," he said, when he recognized me.

"Jack."

We each nodded and humped up our shoulders in our jackets, and I kept walking until we stood side by side looking out at the same dark field.

"How's Ruth?"

"She seems all right. My mother's with her."

He pulled a pipe out of one pocket and set it going. The palms of his hands glowed with the cupped match and looked as translucent as paper. I felt—as I had been lately—that we could all of us go up in an instant. The cloud of smoke settled around him.

"She must've taken a harder fall than I thought," Jack said.

"She gave her head a crack."

"She was bound to, climbing around that way."

"She slipped in her living room," I said.

"Uh hmm."

Jack's smoke shifted into my face and I breathed it in the way I used to breathe in the smell in my grandfather's shirtfront. "She'll be okay," I said.

"What makes you say so?"

I gave him a sharp look, but he didn't notice. "There's no reason to think otherwise," I said, finally.

"No? At her age—at our age, come to that—she's like an old radio, Will. Give it a thump and the tubes smoke up, and the solder breaks here or there, or the wires tangle." He sucked the air in the bottom of the bowl and I heard the tobacco crackle. "She broke something, all right. I was watching her out the kitchen window two mornings back. Want to guess where she was?"

I shook my head, as he was looking at me now.

"Up on her roof. She'd had the Hardwells swarming all over it a month before, so I thought, She's checking their work. Then I thought, *Checking their work!* She's sixty-two years old, Will, but she was perched up on the gable like an owl, peering about as if she was expecting company."

"What sort of explanation did she give you?"

"I never asked her for one."

"You didn't go out?"

"No." His pipe had gone out again, so he held it. "I watched her for nearly an hour until she scrabbled down and hurried inside, looking over her shoulder to see if anyone was watching."

"She didn't see you?"

"In this light, it'd be hard to."

"How long have the two of you been neighbors, Jack?"

He must have been as surprised as I at the accusation in my voice. "I bought this place in 1967, from my uncle," he said. "I know what you're thinking, but you're wrong. I've got as much Christian love in me as any man. I was worried about her, Will, just as you are, and I wanted to go over, but I was—I don't know—hypnotized, or something. She just sat there, turning this way and that like a weather vane, and I just sat watching her the way you would anything unusual, and then she climbed back down, and the spell or whatever it was broke, and then it was too late. It would have been indecent to go over, then."

Neither of us said anything, and the embarrassment between us built until one of us had to go. Being the visitor, I thought it should be me. Jack thought so, too. "'Night," he said, before I was half turned back to Ruth's place.

●   ●   ●

In a town as small as Oracle, our balance is precarious, and
the scales can be tipped with a rumor. It's why most of us
keep our liquor hidden. Before the week was out, I saw that
people in town were giving Ruth a wide berth in stores, or
even on the sidewalk, and it had to be something other than
chance that left an empty space on either end of her old blue
Chevy at the curbs.

Soon it was only my mother who spent any time at all with
her, and then she spent more than she needed to, to keep
the town from tilting. I pretended that she and Ruth had
rekindled an old friendship, as sometimes happens. Oracle,
now, was deep in its autumn gloom, so I'd drive over to Ruth's
in the evening to pick up my mother and take her home.
Walking the one way, in the morning, was enough, she said.
My mother never talked about the day she'd spent—she's
closemouthed anyway—and I never asked, and then I realized that without meaning to I'd gotten like Jack Farley and
had bottled up my curiosity.

Toward the end of October, my mother slid onto the car
seat next to me and said, "Have you heard anything about
Ruth climbing around on her roof?"

"I don't think it's a habit," I said.

"But you've heard something?"

I told her then what Jack had seen.

"He told you that the first day we visited?"

I nodded. "I didn't want to pass on stories," I said. "I fig-
ured if she's getting odd, you'd find out for yourself."

"She's always been odd," my mother said. "Most mornings
when I get there she's sitting buck naked in front of the
television, and she's already got a drink in her hand."

"Well, Christ, Ma."

"Ha!" My mother's voice comes out in a squeak when she
does that. "Ruth's been sitting buck naked with a drink in her
hand in the mornings since I can remember. It used to worry
me a little, sending you over on Saturdays to do her yard."
She squared the purse on her lap. "But climbing her roof is
new, I think."

"Jack said he sat and watched her. He said he was hyp-notized."

"Paint drying would hypnotize Jack Farley."

"At least she wasn't naked," I said.

"She's not crazy, Will."

"I know, Ma."

"She won't hurt anybody."

"No, of course she won't."

My mother was thinking—as I was—of a great-aunt I barely remembered. The family stories had it that she'd taken the inevitable downturn in life with bad grace: when the change had come upon her and she was facing dry age, she'd chased a neighbor two blocks, waving her grandson's Boy Scout hatchet. She'd been naked, too, I recalled.

"Oracle doesn't know that story, anyway," my mother said, reading my mind. "And they don't need to."

"No."

"You've seen her in town, haven't you?"

"Now and again."

"She says she might as well be a stranger for all the atten-tion folks pay her."

"She's right."

"She said she walked into Ed's the other day to pick up some shoes she'd left to be resoled and she had to bang on the counter with her own heels before she got served. And Ed's a cousin."

"That's probably so."

"Why is that, Will?"

"I don't know," I said slowly. "But I guess I feel it, too, maybe." I was thinking about how I'd picked up my mother at Ruth's house every evening for nearly a month without once asking how Ruth was doing, or even if she was still hurting from the headaches, and how quick I'd been to run out into her yard and the dark that first afternoon. It didn't seem to be anything I had any conscious control over. I told her that.

"It's not right," my mother said.

"No," I agreed, and drove her home.

My liquor cabinet is one of the hidden ones. I'd helped my father build his when I was twelve, and I copied a proven design. He'd hidden his behind a piece of paneling; I hid mine in the kitchen behind the false front of a trash compactor. I poured a drink and took it around the house as I turned on lights.

As if I'd invited it, the doorbell rang. It was Jack Farley.

"Will," he said, pulling off his plaid hunting cap and then inhaling the inside air from the front stoop. "Jack Daniel's?"

"Jim Beam," I said. "Come on in, Jack."

"I've been hearing stories," he said when he had a whiskey and a seat.

"About Ruth?"

"About the Hardwells."

"What about them?"

"We're almost into November without an Accident," he said.

"I guess that's right."

"Doesn't that seem odd?"

"They sometimes come late. The Accident of '59 was in March."

"But we always get one."

"We always do, Jack."

Jack smelled his glass, as if he didn't trust it. "Howard Hardwell seems to think there won't be one this year, and it worries him."

"I don't know why it should," I said. "As many Hardwells as we have in Oracle, you'd think it would be an Accident and something awful happening to one of them that would make him worry."

Jack finally took some of his drink. "You don't understand the balance of things, Will."

I thought I did; I'd been thinking a lot about balance, lately, but I nodded for him to go on.

"Don't you see? The Hardwells are sure that Oracle's got to keep falling apart every year so they can keep putting it together."

The Hardwells are our carpenters, gardeners, plumbers,

electricians, and thick-muscled laborers who serve, some-what, as Oracle's glue. I'd never given it much thought be-fore, but they make a very good living at the equinoxes.

"We'll have an Accident, Jack," I said. "Tell Hardwell that."

"We'll have one, one way or another," Jack agreed. "Hard-well will make it happen, I'm sure of it."

"How's Ruth?"

"Who?"

"Ruth Montgomery. Your neighbor."

"Oh." A puzzled look left him. "I don't see her around much anymore. I saw her once up on her roof, did I tell you?"

"I think you told everybody, Jack."

"Maybe so. What's the matter, Will?"

"I don't know." I stood and poured myself another drink and began pacing. "Everything"—all of us—"seems so deli-cate, suddenly. I feel fragile. I feel that a breath of wind could knock us all over."

"Everybody's jittery," Jack said. "It's the waiting." He handed his glass back, still almost full, and turned for the door. "How do you sit with the Hardwells?" he asked.

"Sit with them? I sit with them fine, I suppose."

"That's good," Jack said.

I was still trying to untangle the threat in that when Ruth showed up a half hour later. Thinking it was Jack again, for some reason, and not wanting to talk to him, I looked through the heat-fogged windows before answering the door. It was so dark now that I couldn't even see my sidewalks that I knew to be glazed with ice.

"Your porch light's out," Ruth said when I opened the door.

"Is it? Well, we've got to burn them twenty-four hours a day. Come on in, Ruth."

She shed her coat and sat where Jack had, but after that we were both uncomfortable.

"I wonder if the Hardwells sell them," I said.

"Lightbulbs? Of course they do. They own the hardware store."

"They do?"

"They bought McFarlan out two years ago," she said. "Don't you pay attention?"

"I guess not."

"You can get them in the supermarket, Will. You can get them anywhere."

"I was just thinking about something Jack Farley said about the Hardwells and the Accidents."

"Well, good. I've come to talk to you about the same thing."

"The Hardwells?"

"Jack Farley."

"How about a drink, first?"

"I was afraid you'd make me ask."

When she got it, and when I had another I didn't want, she stared at her drink for a full minute before tasting it. Was something wrong with my liquor? With my glasses?

"Is it all right?"

"Why did Jack Farley come to see you?" she asked instead of answering me.

"He said the Hardwells are nervous."

"They are," she said. "But why did he come to see *you*?"

"I'm not sure."

"Are you friends?"

"Friendly."

"But not friends?"

"No, I guess not."

"He's been to see half a dozen people today," she said. "I've been following him all over town."

"You've been following him." I got the picture I didn't want of her sitting up on her roof.

"He's gone to all of the people who used to be my friends."

"What do you mean, the people who used to be your friends?"

"Stop repeating what I say, Will; it's annoying." She took a long drink and set the glass down, and then leaned forward and put her hands on my knees the way she had with my mother all those long days ago.

I stiffened at the intimacy, and she pulled back, hurt.

"Nobody can see me, Will." She waved a hand back and forth in front of her own eyes. "I'm invisible. I went to see your mother this morning, following Jack's trail, and she had trouble remembering who I was."

"She's known you most of her life. All of mine," I said.

"It was like she was—I don't know."

"Hypnotized?"

"Maybe."

"I'll go see her."

She touched me again, and I shrank from her again. "It's not her, Will. It's me."

"But I know who you are."

"Yes, that's curious. I half expected you to stand in the door and ask me what I wanted."

"I can't believe it's as bad as you say."

"It's worse." She spun the glass in her hands so the ice rattled. "I think it has something to do with that fall I took. Is that crazy?"

I'd forgotten about that. "How are your headaches?" I asked.

"They're gone," she said. "They stopped just after your mother quit visiting"—she laughed—"but don't tell her that. And I'm not cold anymore, at least no colder than I should be, no colder than—" She clamped her mouth shut and then brought the glass up to it.

"No colder than what?"

"Than everybody else is."

Into that pause I finally inserted a question about Jack Farley. "You were following him when we left off," I reminded her.

"He's been going from house to house, to my old friends," she said. "I track him to the next place and then go back to the last place, but when I knock they don't know me."

"He came here."

"I know that, Will. What did he say about me?"

"What makes you think he said anything about you?" I didn't tell her that Jack hardly knew who she was.

"Didn't he?"

"No. He came to tell me that the Hardwells are going to cause some sort of accident if we don't get one of the real ones."

"There's been an Accident, Will," she said. "It's happened to me."

"You slipped."

"No." She shook her head, and when she looked up at me I thought she'd cry. "I slipped away." She put her glass down and got into her coat, and shoved her hands deep into her pockets. She looked me right in the eyes. "I found Jack Farley staring into my bedroom window last night," she said. "His eye didn't stop on me, or the bed, or the television, or on anything; it was as if he were staring into an empty house."

"Ruth."

"He's always wanted my place," she said. "Now I'm afraid he'll buy it—that the bank will sell it to him—while I'm still living there."

"Ruth."

She straightened and smiled weakly. "Do me a favor? Meet me downtown tomorrow at lunchtime and let me show you something?"

"Sure."

At the door, she turned and bussed my cheek. "What's my last name, Will?" she whispered shyly.

When I couldn't answer, she nodded and left.

She put an arm through mine in the drugstore the next day, surprising me, and marched me up to the pharmacy counter. Abe had just finished ringing up a sale, and after he handed Mrs. Drummond her change, Ruth centered herself so he'd have to look around her at me.

"Hi, Will," he said. "Something I can get for you?"

I felt her grip tighten.

"I think"—what was her name?—"this woman wants something," I said. A panic stirred in me.

"Fine. Send her in to see me."

"*This* woman," I repeated, and tugged my arm to free it.

"Who?"

I couldn't remember. I couldn't turn to look at her, afraid that I really might be standing alone. Her weight on my arm was light. Something crossed Abe's face—concern, or impatience—and when it did I shook her loose for good and reached into my pocket for a quarter. "Excuse me," I said, and ran for the phone.

Out of the corner of my eye, I saw a flat, fuzzy image, like an old photograph, and then just Abe. I had to call Jack. Don't let the Hardwells do it, I wanted to tell him. Oracle's had its Accident, and it's happened to all of us.

THE MOVABLE HAZARD

The game is played in Scotland while leaning into a head wind and bowed in a reverential hush. Great golfers have breathed here. The game was inspired here. And sprites inspired it. They're cousins to the wee folk of Ireland, but more imaginative. While leprechauns are rather tightfisted, mean-minded little bastards, sprites are friendly, easygoing elves, a bit like undergraduates. The Irish and the Scots somehow got by accident each other's fairy tales.

Originally, sprites inhabited the western shore of Scotland, where the prevailing winds drive the ocean onto the rocks. At first they lived just in that margin where the two collide, cruelly buffeted, but one of their number by dint of exploration (another story) discovered up the coast a kilometer or two a bay, and in that bay a cove, and edging that cove a beach of fine sand. And it was sand above all else that golf needed that it might be conceived. For, tangled rough and horrible weather aside, what's golf without a trap?

Unless it's water.

Those sprites are fairly nervous if the ocean's not near. If every course were laid out like the first links, only the Scots would hate themselves enough to play it, for each hole fronted the ocean: nearly four miles of potentially unplayable lies. The Scots—painting themselves blue five hundred years later and calling themselves Picts—gave it to the Romans as a gift in return for their invasion, and one story has it that the game was taken back to Rome and the empire was in ruins in a generation. The first golfers had the Firth of Clyde on the right hand—if they sliced—and the left hand—if they hooked—and a strip of bumpy ground down the center that had been dug up here and there and filled with sand. (Trees were added later by the leprechauns; Scotland has no trees.)

"Och, *gowf*," an old Scot said, and played it with pleasure, and then went back to his dark smokey hovel and beat himself about the head and shoulders with a gnarled stick (for pleasure).

In the old days, sprites would gather in small multitudes and sit along the fairways (that is, on the rocks, near the ocean) in tiny galleries, and if a ball came near, one of them would jump up and kick it into the sea. A golf ball and a sprite are exactly the same size, but the balls then were made of feathers and so for them it was a manly sport, a cross between soccer and badminton. It wasn't unusual to see a golfer chasing a sprite with his brassie or cleek, trying mightily to put *him* close to the pin. You don't see them around much anymore—sprites, I mean—as the balls nowadays are hard and heavy enough to decimate a family. The game they invented because they hated the Scots has come around to make them fearful for their lives.

It's only fair.

Still, they'll get up to a spot of mischief, now and then.

Claude Armstrong, a distant cousin to his more famous relative, Jack, having grown up in Ohio, where the fairways are flat and smooth and oceans are on postcards, thought he'd travel to Mecca to play golf. He had a four handicap, which is low enough to make a man want—need, rather—to play St. Andrews.

The State Department should not allow Americans to go to Scotland if they are golfers. Claude Armstrong took the train up from London and thought he'd warm up on courses around Ayr and Kilmarnock before he pushed on to martyrdom and glory. He came to Linx, a small village on the rocky western shore that has been forgotten by men as the site of the first golf course. Fourteen holes are spread out along the ocean.

The tiny hamlet of Linx has sixty souls (none playing to higher than a ten) and three pubs, and Claude chose one called The Brandished Club because he liked its name and the painting of a white-whiskered, bekilted old man with a raised stick, and because it was the first one he came to. He pushed pipe smoke to the sides and found a table at the window. (That table was unoccupied because Scots, like gnomes, prefer dark, warm, cave-like recesses, and summer was blowing through that front window in a gale.)

"A pint of your best bitter," Claude told the innkeeper, "and directions out to the links, if you please. I'd like to scare up a caddie, too, if I can."

The innkeeper stared uncomprehendingly. He understood *bitter* and *Linx,* and he made sense out of *caddie,* but the rest was a muddle. He shook his head and served Claude a beer and sorted through the change held out in an open palm until he'd got what he wanted.

Rain began to lash the front window, and Claude frowned, and then the publican spotted his clubs and understood.

"It's *gowf* you're wantin'," he said.

Claude nodded sadly.

"A bonny day fer't."

"Bonny? This?"

"Aye." The innkeeper squinted at the light coming in. "Soomer."

"What?"

"August." He made it sound like *aghast.* "I've a wee lad that'll caddie fer ye handsome."

"A wee lad?"

The innkeeper held his hand out, waist high, about three feet. "He's yoong, an' only playin' to a nine, but he knows the links. He'll take ye a-boot fine."

So the innkeeper brought out his son Colin and paired him with Armstrong. The boy wrestled Claude's bag over one shoulder and said, "C'mon, sure," and was out into the pelting rain before Claude could rise from his chair.

"Hi'it straight," the innkeeper called after him.

The first thing an American golfer in Scotland learns is that he can't count on the yardages he's used to with his clubs. The same ball, the same club; but a seven won't go 150 yards. A four might. A three will, most times, unless it's summer breezes you're fighting, and then you need a fairway wood.

Colin led Claude to the 1st tee and pointed through the downpour at the flag. "Two seventy-five," he said.

Short par four, Claude thought. A chance at eagle.

But he was on in four, and three-putted for a seven. He'd taken his driver off the tee and connected in his usual fashion, but in the heavy air of Scotland (what else explained it?) his ball flew 185 yards instead of the expected 270. It landed exactly in the center of the fairway and then rolled with the contours into one of the wrinkles that hid under the short grass.

"What's the rule here?" he asked Colin, seeing his ball wedged into a crevice.

"Rule?"

"A drop, I suppose. Is this ground under repair?"

"Ye play it as it lies, sure," the boy said.

Claude had to play it out sideways *into* the rough *from* the fairway. "This is madness," he said.

"Aye," said Colin. *"Gowf."*

He had ninety yards to the pin. He reached for his pitching wedge.

"There's nae wrong wi' tha' if ye've the arms of me father," Colin said, "but it's a mighty blast ye're wantin'."

"Ninety yards?" Claude said. "With a wedge?"

"Aye."

"What do you suggest, son?"

"An eight should put ye right."

"An *eight*?"

"I've only seen ye hi' the ba' twice't," the boy said, backing away. "Ye might know best all the same."

Now he was between clubs. He wouldn't think twice about the shot normally, but he remembered a good drive from the tee that had come up well short, and he remembered the innkeeper saying his son played "only to a nine" and that he knew the links. Maybe a nine would be right.

"What's behind the green?" he asked.

"Th' Atlantic," the boy said.

Now he was between clubs again. "There's got to be something between the green and the ocean."

"Oh, aye. *Rr*rocks."

"I'll have the wedge after all."

The boy gave it to him with the same resignation all children have toward the actions of adults. Claude swung it and hit a towering shot that stopped dead at the top of its arc and dropped straight down, forty yards short. He chipped on with his seven iron from there, to the boy's belated approval.

The green was all humps and much faster than it should have been in that rain. Claude felt good about getting down in three from twenty feet.

"Tough greens."

"Gowf," the boy said.

They went on to the 2nd. The 2nd was again a straightaway par four along the ocean that looked innocent to Claude. The only trouble he could see was a bunker in the fairway about two hundred yards out, but with the same wind in his face, Claude knew he'd never reach it.

Still, unnerved by the 1st, he asked, "Any trouble I don't see?"

"That boonker," the boy said.

"You think I can reach it?"

"Aye."

"Isn't it two hundred yards?"

"Aye."

"With the same wind against?"

"Aye."

"What should I hit, then?"

Colin shrugged. "It does nae matter."

Claude, exasperated, asked for his three iron. He knew that would be well short, but would leave him, at the most, an-

other three to get home. He'd play this hole safe and take—
at worst—a par.

He hit a good shot into the wind, maybe 160 yards, but the
ball came down in the bunker.

"That's impossible."

"They all say tha' th' firs' time," Colin said, and started off
the tee with Claude's bag.

"Wait a minute. That bunker's not two hundred yards."

"That bunker's where it needs to be," Colin said.

"Give me my driver, and a ball."

Colin kept his head down and did as he was asked.

Claude drove his second ball long and true, nearly 200
yards, and the ball came down in the bunker.

Disbelief gave way to determination. "Give me an eight
iron," he told his caddie. "And another ball."

That shot, maybe 110 yards, came down in the bunker.

"'Fore ye hit again, sure, ta' another o' the tee wi' the long
stick. Ye'll be tha' much closer t' the green."

Sure enough, when Claude drove his fourth shot with his
driver, his ball—in the bunker—was only a short iron from
the flag.

"Playin' seven from the boonker," the boy said.

"It's not possible to get off this tee without landing in that
bunker," Claude said.

"Aye. It's worse on fourteen," the boy said, "wi' the hazard."

Claude played the other holes in a daze, taking whatever
club the boy offered and knocking it down or lobbing it not as
logic and weather demanded, but as Colin suggested.

"Fair gowf," the boy said, after 13, "fer a rough beginnin'."

"This is the last hole?"

"Aye. We ne'er built past this."

"I'm surprised you built past the third," Claude said.

"Now, sure, that hazard moves," Colin said, pointing.

"It moves."

"Aye."

The hazard under discussion was a brackish salt marsh no
larger than a duck pond. It bisected the fairway a middle iron

from the tee, and under normal circumstances Claude wouldn't have hesitated to drive over it.

"It *moves,* you say?"

Colin nodded apologetically.

"Whatever I hit, I'll be in that marsh?"

"Aye. Unless ye drive it into the sea."

"What if I drive it onto the green?"

Colin looked at Armstrong as if he were mad. "It's been done onc't," he said, slowly, "so legend has it."

The 14th was a par five of 420 yards, straightaway like all the rest, with the ocean on the right.

"The wind's agin'," the boy reminded him.

"Is it ever away?" Claude asked.

"Just that onc't."

"So," Claude said, "two great shots, but one of them in the hazard, and you're on in three, no matter what?"

The boy puzzled through that. "It's a par five," he said, as if to say, "What do you expect?"

"That fellow that got on in one," Claude said, "what happened?"

"Two-putted for eagle," Colin said, "an' deed a *rr*ruined mon."

"How so?"

"Our pixies," Colin said seriously. "Th' sprites."

"Sprites?"

Colin nodded. "Tha' marsh is to remind men of the border 'tween water an' land. Ye'll land in the muck o' the shore of it. Ye can nae miss it."

"What would happen," Claude asked slowly, "if I were to walk a ball out to just past the hazard, where you know I could drive it, and then play my second from there?"

"D'ye mean *cheat*?"

"No, but . . . well—"

"That's nae *gowf,* Mister A*rr*mst*rr*ong." And with that, Colin dropped Claude's bag and walked away, shaking his head sadly so that water sprayed from it in a halo.

Claude watched him go. As if the boy were himself a low-pressure center, the rain went with him and the sun came out. The grass glittered like jewels. Then the wind dropped, stopped, and began to back around.

"Come back!" Claude yelled, but Colin was too far.

In no time at all, Claude Armstrong had a stiff wind behind, and the 420 yards seemed nearly reachable. A low drive that rises slowly, with some topspin, and these miraculously hard fairways . . .

Sprites gathered in the weeds of the marsh, as at a funeral, and looked sadly back at the tee.

Claude powdered his ball.

It was a low, boring drive that rose slowly, with topspin, and, on these hard fairways, when it hit sixty yards short, it shot forward and rolled up next to the pin. His cry of joy rang from the rocks. When he got to the green, he read the putt from all angles and with a superhuman effort steadied his sudden nervousness and knocked the six-footer in for double eagle. He'd never in his life even *seen* a double eagle.

His legs were shaking from the walk and his groin chafed from the wet, but he was exuberant when he sat back down at his old table at The Brandished Club.

"Buy everybody another of what they're having," he told the innkeeper.

A Scots cheer went up: a murmur, and raised glasses, and raised eyebrows.

"Ye've a good round, then. Where's the lad?"

"He isn't back?"

The innkeeper shook his head.

"I double-eagled fourteen," Claude said.

"Ye din nae."

"I did."

Claude thought the noise and the sudden silence that followed it was a gunshot, but then he realized that every man in the pub had put his heavy pewter tankard down on the wooden tables at the same time. The hush was so complete that Claude thought he could hear pulses.

"I did," he said again. "I drove the green to six feet of the pin."

"Where's the boy?"

"I don't know. He left before I finished."

"*Ah.*" Like a let breath, the tankards came up again.

"None but Stuart Hagar e'er drove the fourteenth," the innkeeper said. "Ye'd do well t' save yer stories fer yer home-comin'."

"He's the one died a ruined man?"

"An' nearly too' the village wi' him."

"Because he drove the fourteenth green?"

"Aye." The publican drew a half-pint of bitter for himself and sat down with Claude. "It's the refusal, here," he said, tapping his own heart, "t' land in tha' marsh and pay 'omage to the wee ones that's the crime. An' they'll curse men fer't."

"Curse?"

"Aye. Stuart's cattle deed, then his wife an' bairns, an' then he lost a leg an' an arm an' an ee."

"Ee?"

The innkeeper pointed to his eye. "He couldn't *gowf.* Worse, he din nae want to."

"Cattle an' sheep deed all a-boot," said a voice from the dark recesses of the pub, like a priest or a poet in the old days, Claude thought.

"An' a pestilence swept all thro' the town."

"It nearly got us all," the innkeeper said.

"When was this?"

"Fifteen hundert an' ninety-three," the innkeeper said. "God rest us."

"Jesus," Claude said, "that's four hundred years ago."

"Th' good Lord willin'."

"That's nonsense."

After another deadly silence, Claude heard the ringing of coins on tabletops, a sound rarely heard in Scotland.

"They'll nae ha' yer drinks after all," the innkeeper said. "Ye'r nae welcome here."

And so Claude Armstrong, backing out as he'd seen men do

in B westerns, went up the road and played the St. Andrews old course at one under par, and then went back to America and played Pebble Beach.

He was playing the 18th of that religious place, with the wind against, when his ball drew over the rocks and landed on a narrow strip of beach between the sea and the western shore. His three playing partners, having the worst rounds of their lives, silently applauded. None had a handicap over ten, and each had already a score over 100.

The tide was out, and the ball playable. "I want to play it," he said.

"Go ahead," said his partners, in unison.

Claude Armstrong went down.

But he slipped on a rock and landed hard on his left side, wedged in a crevice. A numbness struck him in that arm and leg, and his vision in his left eye blurred. He thought he saw tiny people and thought he heard tiny voices.

"Ye'll play great gowf the rest' o' yer days," a voice said, "an' all ye play wi' will hate ye fer't. Ye'll be a hazard to yer partners, an' ye'll end yer life playin' alone."

And his vision came back, and the feeling in his limbs, and he stood over his ball on the beach and hit a marvelous three iron to the pin, where it dropped for double eagle.

PEEPER

The boy begins his summer planning crimes. If he's ten, almost eleven, trouble's voice is sweeter than a choir's, and he knows he will be forgiven any misstep that doesn't end in murder. A boy ten-going-on-eleven is havoc's darling.

Brought to summary justice at one sidewalk court or another, he'll stand before his accusers in a T-shirt and holed jeans, wearing his innocence in tousled hair, freckles, and bare feet. And if it turns out that he's wrong about this—that the schoolteacher's wife or the grocer sees through his simple disguise—his father has taught him that a lie will fit his mouth as comfortably as a river stone curls in his hand.

In that first dark before light after the last of school, he lies awake thinking, following as if from a height the map of the town that he keeps in his head. The truth rises like smoke from that imagined landscape, and he nods to himself: mornings are for stealing.

He slides from his bed like oil and steps into his clothes, a shrug and a zip and a snap. Out the window, on the fire escape, the crosshatched metal grating is already warm under his feet, springing a little under his weight. He sucks in a breath as only a boy facing summer can, and the good smell of bricks fills his nose. The wall is like sandpaper to his touch. The first pink, like an embarrassment, has caught the top floor of the hotel.

"Thievery," he whispers. It's either a promise or a description.

He waits on the third-floor landing until the dark and light are in equal parts, when the air shimmers like glass, and then he runs down the laddered stairs to the sidewalk and ducks under the window where his father is sitting out the end of his shift on the night desk. Facts appear in front of his eyes like print on letterhead stationery:

Hotel Bucklin
Elkhart, Indiana

5 June, 1940

The sheet of paper in his mind breaks apart but confirms his belief that he is living a memory not yet made but in the making, that he will remember on his deathbed the smells and colors of this morning, the feel of the brick against his fingers, the temperature of the sidewalk under his bare feet. He accepts this easily, the way boys acknowledge from birth the inevitable certainty of destiny. He turns left, runs down an alley, and at the end of it he shouts once, not in language but in an inarticulate hieroglyphic of joy.

Take something, anything.

At the end of the block a small, half-formed pyramid lies tumbled, its stone sheaves tied with twine. The boy has his two-bladed pocket knife jacked open and is cutting before he is bent over, has the top edition in his hand before the knife snicks through, and is around the corner just as the other boys arrive in a loose knot to claim their goods.

He unfolds it.

DUNKIRK BEACHES NOW GERMAN

The headline swims and then settles into a syntax he understands. He reads just enough to know that he wants to be there too, with those defeated men, rocking in the oily swell in small boats and watching the town behind them burn. Gee whiz. Stealing an *army.* He'll be old enough in ten years for the landing at Inchon and another retreat (from the Chongchon River, in freezing cold), but he doesn't know that now.

He's over there, somewhere off the coast of France, worrying about submarines and fussing with the wind's direction and the morning light, shifting both of them first this way and then the other before deciding that the wind is blowing out, offshore, carrying the thick black smoke to the boats. A newsboy walks through it, settling a loaded sandwich bag over his shoulders, leaning into its weight of rolled newspapers stacked like artillery rounds. "Hey, Cleve," the boy says.

"Hey, Tom."

The newspaper is forgotten in Cleve's hand. He watches with something like jealousy as Tom crosses the street and tosses a paper against Mr. Willmont's hardware store window.

A car starts up, someone grinds a gear, it pulls away. The day is beginning and Cleve has wasted its most precious half-hour.

He trails behind Tom, watching him, a block distant, reach and throw, reach and throw, the newspapers grenades now, the shrubbery and porches blown to bits where they land. Flame curls like handwriting out of the smoke. All thoughts of theft have flown.

It's an accident that determines his life. Tom has thrown Cherry Street and has turned onto Third. Cleve, halfway up the block, is skinning his feet against the buckled sidewalks and blaming himself for ruining the first day of summer. He hears the hinge of a screen door, stops, and looks sideways. A hedge hides him to his shoulders. A man in a robe and slippers is bending down to pick up the paper Tom has thrown, and behind him in a lit hallway is his wife, wearing only a pair of her husband's boxer shorts. Cleve has never seen a woman's breasts. He's imagined them a thousand times, but he's never guessed they look like round white targets with red bull's-eyes painted on them. The man stabs at her between the legs with the rolled paper and she laughs and then the door bangs closed and Cleve is left standing at the hedge with his hands in his pockets and that picture of her burned into his eyes.

•   •   •

Full dark, now. He's spent the day hoping for enough heat to make trees limp. His father is down at the night desk, probably counting the revolutions of the fan's slowly spinning propellers, the warm air from it eddying around the hot room but not even stirring the calendar pages.

It's so easy he wonders why he's never thought of it. The Hotel Bucklin on the outside is all fire escapes and ledges, and barefooted he is as sure as a goat.

He carries on a string, slung like a rifle over his back, the periscope he made last year out of a cardboard tube and pieces of his father's shaving mirror. From the roof, balancing on the parapet, he hopes it will give him an upside-down look into the fifth-floor windows.

He doesn't often go to the roof. It's hot tar paper and broken glass. Guy wires are strung randomly, invisible in the dark. He'd been up here a year ago, at the end of the summer, when a drunk had stumbled up through the inside stairs, shouting, shadowboxing, and hurling empty bottles he'd brought with him in a paper sack. One of them had struck Cleve on a carom, and his yell of pain and fear and surprise had brought the drunk after him, suspicious and deadly. Cleve had escaped him, gone down the stairs, and told his father, and his father, after checking to see that the boy was all right, had given him a hiding for being where he shouldn't and for being a slow target.

Cleve walks carefully now, sliding his feet along because of the glass no one has swept up, burning them on the tarpaper and asphalt, holding his hands in front to intercept wires. He half hopes to see the drunk again, passed out or dead (maybe dead a long time) (this last winter perhaps) (frozen first and then thawed and now rotting), but the roof is empty. He unslings his periscope, lies flat on the cement edge, and inches it down.

Battleship is his thought. She's enormous. A gauzy yellow curtain hangs in the window, and the room is nearly dead dark behind it, just the orange glow from a radio dial like a flashlight about to give up, but Cleve can see her like it is day.

"I got X-ray eyes," he says to himself quietly in the deep voice he uses to describe himself. "I can look through curtains and bedroom walls like Superman."

She isn't completely naked; she has wrapped herself in more of that curtain material and is lying on a sofa bed with her knees apart because of the heat. Upside-down like this, reflected in a pair of mirrors, she looks like a full meal set underneath a tablecloth.

She rolls sideways to get up and Cleve thinks of torpedoed ships capsizing. He rolls sideways, too, back onto the roof, and breathes shallowly from an excitement that has nothing to do with her.

It takes him nearly three hours to work his way around the hotel's fifth floor. Most of the rooms are empty (either that, or he can't really see through bedroom walls after all). His feet are burned. His stomach, too. His shoulders twitch and jump from holding the periscope over the ledge at such a strange angle.

He decides to peep the other floors another night, falls naked into bed, and covers himself with a sheet. He has marvelous dreams that he can't afterward remember.

The second day of summer is like waking to a life he's born to. He rises in the dark with a purpose. The map in his head glows with street names and house numbers and the best places of concealment.

Being on the loose in a small town before dawn is as close to holy as a boy can get. Look: he scrawls an obscene picture (using his newfound half-knowledge) on a windshield with a piece of soapstone he carries for just such things; he urinates onto a manhole cover in the middle of town; he runs naked down the middle of a quiet street with his jeans in one hand, his T-shirt in the other; he is invisible, invulnerable, ineluctable. His life's path gleams with inevitability: he's a boy prophet, a boy spy, a boy soldier; he's a boy the world is going to have to reckon with.

Miss Harwood, the fourth-grade teacher whose class he's just escaped, is going to have to reckon with Cleve first. She is the woman who makes him uncomfortable when he's near her, yet the woman he found himself next to accidentally or not-so-accidentally three or four times a day. It is her bedroom light that he spots from the street, and her dew-damp yard that he prowls now as the sky turns pearly.

He climbs a thick-limbed, white-barked tree until he is standing on air head-high outside her window. With an easy, cross-armed nonchalance, she pulls a lacy nightshift up over her head and turns to look right through him, then bends over a bureau drawer to pull out underthings. She is freckled, redheaded, and slim.

Now he knows what the bottom half looks like: it looks unfinished. There seems to be a mile between her belly button and the triangle where her legs join, and with nothing covered, her legs aren't all that pretty. She steps into pale blue panties and pulls them up, which is better, and then straps herself into her brassiere. Better still. She palms her breasts and rubs them into place with one quick, half-circular motion. Like turning a crank.

He slides down and finds another window. By the time it is full light, he has peeped three bedrooms, and he has found out already this early in his career that he likes to watch women dressing or undressing, but not naked.

At the end of that summer there isn't a woman in Elkhart he hasn't watched.

In 1950, he goes to Korea.

His childhood has given him a variety of slinking skills, and the army is quick to take advantage. He ends up walking long point. He's a scout.

Nobody climbs trees faster, sees better at night, finds and counts—and shoots—the enemy at longer range. His sergeant tells him he has X-ray eyes. If the Chinese send women to fight, he thinks, he can have the war won in a month.

His helmet freezes to his hair, and his socks to his feet. His boots to his socks. His skin to his bones. He carries Indiana inside him like canned heat, but at times he thinks it's no more than a hallucination that he's known a place that's warm.

On the long retreat to the thirty-eighth parallel, those at
point become the rear guard, as his division was the first in.
He believes himself to be the whitest boy in this white landscape, the American deepest in a place none of them belong.
And he's right.

It's all right in the daylight hours. The Chinese are hidden,
gone. It's a frozen, empty place in the day, except in front of
him, where the road is clogged with tired men and heavy,
muddy guns. The army could have back the ground they'd
lost the night before, if they wanted it. But there's no thought
of that.

It's at night that the Chinese do their work, like wolves,
sneaking up to softball-pitching distance before they open
fire, and it is at night that Cleve herds the men he is with into
triangular formations, nipping at their heels like a sheepdog,
directing their fire to where the enemy is not yet, but coming. He is able to distinguish shades of black and find the
moving one in all that unmoving place.

He gets a medal for this, later, and another one for carrying
a friend a hundred yards under fire. But more importantly to
Cleve, he gets out with his skin.

Somebody behind the lines he doesn't even know hands
him a favor—that's how it is in war—and he ends up in Seoul
around Christmas for a long three weeks. Here, stripping as
an industry is already flourishing, a service to the American
army, and although he pays and watches with all the other
boys from the Midwest, it holds no interest for him. Clothed
or naked, even the Korean women over forty remind him of
little girls, and he is no pedophile.

He remembers that summer day in Elkhart he knows he
can never forget, and even remembers the headline on the
newspaper he stole, and he has the sense to think that sometimes you should be careful what you wish for.

He's sitting at a wicker table holding half a warm beer and
watching still another prostitute sit on still another GI's lap.
The soldier drives one hand up between her legs under her
tight chong-sam and another between the buttons at her

chest, and Cleve comes to the conclusion that war, despite all its other horrors, mostly just sucks the dignity out of everybody.

In 1960, he's arrested for the first time. This happens in Tupelo, Mississippi, where during the day he sells Oldsmobiles.

The police in Tupelo are not so much concerned that he has broken the law as they are offended that somebody would peep their women. And disgusted that he'd be peeping Negroes. "Get a good look at that nigger bitch?" he is asked just before he's hit.

He's pushed into the back of a Ford Fairlane already crowded with other beaten suspects, the reason the police are in this part of town to begin with. "This one's lookin' through windows at your women," the deputy says, and three pairs of swollen, dark eyes swell up even more. The man nearest to him hisses like a cat. His tongue is bright pink.

He's relieved when they put him in a cell by himself, but less relieved when they take him back out of that and into a room for questioning and he sees the deputy pulling on gloves.

"Yep," the deputy says. "These are so I get answers."

"I'll answer anything," Cleve says.

"Yep, that's so."

His overnight incarceration in that Mississippi jail scars his face so badly that he'll ever afterwards look like the monster they say he is. He never gets all the vision back in his left eye and from then on has to peep what he thinks of as right-hand windows.

In 1970, he's arrested for the 114th time, and this time they put him in a hospital.

He's in California, just outside San Diego. The beatings are administered with electricity instead of fists, with boredom instead of indignation, and he finds himself at odd times of the day in a chaise longue in the garden, staring up into the green hearts of palm trees without any memory of how he got

there. The *rachety-rachety-rachety-rachety* of a sprinkler reminds him of small-caliber weapons, and everybody, even the
patient sitting next to him, is dressed in white. He has trouble
sorting it all out.

"Now, Mr. Hanran?"

"Yes?"

"You've been arrested one hundred and fourteen times?"

"Yes. About that, I guess. If that's what it says."

"For lewd and lascivious behavior."

"For peeping."

"You look in windows?"

"Through the curtains."

"Ah. Do you think women leave the curtains open for you?"
The doctor slashes at the air with his hand, making a vertical
slit.

"I look *through* the curtains."

"Do you expose yourself?"

"No."

"Masturbate?"

"No. Well, not right then."

"But later?"

"Sure. Sometimes. Don't you?"

Then he's in the garden again.

"What do you remember of your mother?"

"Nothing. Almost nothing."

Then he's in the garden again.

"Tell me what you think of this picture."

Then he's in the garden again.

When he is released he has twenty-one dollars and seven-
teen cents and a Bronze Star in the pockets of a pair of plaid
pants he doesn't remember buying.

In 1980 he's putting civilian airplanes together in a hangar
the size of a city block in Everett, Washington. There are
women everywhere, and he undresses them while he works.
It's not much, but it's something. He's glad his hands know

somehow what to do and that in some other place the parts he joins are X-rayed.

A decade or most of it goes by and Cleve takes the first job that comes his way, which is night clerk at the Hotel Bucklin.

"She's not going to last much longer," the manager says.

"Oh?"

"Six months. A year. She's falling apart, and no one's got the money to fix her."

"I grew up here," Cleve says, but the man doesn't seem to hear him. "In this same hotel. My dad had this job when I was a boy."

He settles into the chair at the desk his first night and wonders what's become of his parents. They're both dead, certainly; either that, or nearly ninety. Some news of his father hums in his head like an insect, but doesn't land. No news of his mother has ever landed.

The night goes slowly. People in jobs like this—in jobs like he's had all his life, he thinks—feel every passing second. If they work at night, they're even forced to wait for the next second to come around. Selling cars is like this. Building airplanes is like this. His father must have been two or three hundred years old when he gave it up.

In the early hours, when nothing at all in town is moving, when even the drunks have stopped drinking, he feels the weight of those sleeping in the hotel above his head. He imagines he hears bedsprings when a body rolls over.

When the morning man comes on at six, Cleve buys breakfast at the diner and then roams the town. Elkhart is the same as he left it. The hardware store's still there, but part of a chain now. The paperboys pick up on the same corner. Old trees still shade the same streets, and boys on their way to school are still at their same games.

He'd forgotten what small-town Indiana smells like in the spring. Every blade of grass, every flower, every leaf on every tree is warring to out-perfume the others. It's Monday, and the lawns are new-mown. Cars are starting up, here and there, and even their exhaust is sweet.

America. Foreign places rush into his head, fighting for a place in his memory, and he sees odd, transposed pictures of snow and dark water and palm trees, lying one on top of the other like a palimpsest. He sees the insides of hospitals and jails and bedrooms. He sees his old dad under a slowly turning propeller back in the job he just left, and a long-dead drunk—half a century dead, now—on the roof of the Hotel Bucklin. Slated for demolition, the manager said.

Pretty, young women are leaving their homes and getting into their cars for work. When did this happen? Why aren't the men going to work? Maybe they are, he thinks. Maybe he's standing in a swarm of them, ghosts that exist in another dimension. Half the world invisible to his failing vision.

In two weeks—no more than that—he can't stand it anymore, so at three in the morning he takes the keys from the desk. He smells the dust that his soft footfalls bring up from the faded floral carpets. He slides a key into a lock. He's too old, after all, to be climbing around on fire escapes.

The room he steals into is dark and smells of chalk. The woman is middle-aged, maybe forty-five, and large, and snoring. She kicks gently in her dreams. He stands over her for a moment and then brings in a chair from another room and places it by her bed and sits down and crosses his legs and waits for the morning.

GARDENER

A spider's shadow thrown hugely on a white wall looms suspended on unseen cords. I look for the shadow-thrower. I find it only by an accident of motion: a pale yellow- and cream-colored spider, hanging nearly invisible on a morning string, is poised above my coffee. I blow on it, and it sways, dangling as it does between fate and chance. I am neither, I decide, and leave it alone.

My old cat with his blind eyes lies curled at my feet in the sun, blinking at what he can't see and swatting his tail in discontent or dreams. It's hard to tell when that cat's asleep, as he often forgets to close his eyes.

I run a finger between his ears. He stirs, blinks, and tilts his head back until I can look down his ear canals—not lavender, and not pink—and then he folds his ears back and I stare into those peach-colored eyes, white now and forever with cataracts. It's a glossy, glassy sheen like watered silk that's unpleasant to look at, but it bothers me, probably, more than it does the cat.

Rising heat makes little wavy lines. I sit at the barbecue, as avocado-shaped as the cat. He gets up every hour or so to stretch and examine again his thirty feet of garden. To him it is most likely different each time, but to me it looks always the same. He comes back and lies at my feet like a dog.

If I look up, I can see the city pressed around us in heat-bent lines, but I prefer to stare instead into the cat's small jungle (I leave it wild), or into his blind eyes, or into the glowing coals of the barbecue. The cat and I together are gentle, old, tame.

Alice found us this way, in these same sitting positions, the day before last.

"Tony," she said, "you can't go on living in your backyard."

She always says that, or something like it. It's one of her directives that she stabs out from time to time.

"I can," I said. "I do, when I'm not working."

"And that cat of yours should be put down." She dabbed at something near her eye with her little finger. "Poor thing."

"The cat's happy. I am, too."

"You can't be."

Alice has her mind made up. She is a frail woman, and the same age as I, but on the inside *she* is iron.

She chose the best of the lawn chairs and sat. "Tell me, Tony," she said, and then said nothing.

That is one of her tricks. I am on to all of them. I said nothing, too.

"This inheritance of yours," she said, and let it hang.

"Um hum?"

"You have it now, don't you?"

"Um hum."

"Is that a yes?"

"That's a yes, yes, Alice."

"Well, then?"

Here I was supposed to jump up and agree to move out of the city—to Connecticut, I think—and to buy things. All sorts of large, expensive things. That's all Alice wants of me. I continue to resist her, but I haven't much resistance left. My life is of more consequence to Alice than it is to me.

"Tony?"

"Yes."

"Why don't you move?"

"Why don't I buy things?"

"Exactly. It's not normal." She crossed one stockinged leg

over the other and smoothed her skirt. Women in skirts look ridiculous in lawn chairs, and she knew it.

"There's nothing much I want, Alice, except to be left alone. You know that, yet you keep pestering."

"It's for your own good, dear."

The funny thing is, I hardly know her. She's the friend of a dead aunt—and of my late wife, she tells me—and she's wormed her way into the family, and the family's business, through years of lawn parties and bridge games. That's why, I guess, I never noticed her much. I tell myself she would never have bothered with us if somebody in the family didn't have some money, but I may be mistaken.

"I'm always like this," I said. "I always have been."

"Isn't that the truth." She got up to go. "You really should get away from here, Tony dear, it's so depressing. It's so—" funereal, she wanted to say, but didn't.

"Attack," I told the cat, but he curled up and exposed his chin, wanting a rub.

When Alice had gone I had no choice but to think of the money. It never quite goes away—the thought of money—but the spirit of it hangs so intensely around Alice that other people simply have no other option but to think of it when she's near. She has the smell of it about her, as other women do perfume.

My inheritance is more of an allowance than a fortune. It is enough for me to move, if I want, and quit working, if I live modestly. It surely won't buy all the things that Alice has in mind. I'm uncomfortable with it because an inheritance—or an allowance, for that matter—seems awkward at sixty.

The spider spins in a crotch of the tree. It's a she-spider, I am certain. Speckled tummy and long, brown legs. She weaves, and weaves, her geometry worse each time; she leaves holes in her design like the empty spaces in lace, but randomly, perhaps from the pesticides and fertilizers that she sucks from her victims. If so, they've gotten them somewhere else.

The cat has gone off to explore a smell. It was nearly visible, the way it came to him: his whiskers stiffened, his nose twitched. His head came up swiveling like a radar dish. His ears curled forward, and he flicked his tongue out to taste it, and then he moved off, not yet standing, but growing taller as he walked through the long grass and worked his way into the dark shadows where I can't follow him. Won't follow him.

I add a handful of briquettes to the fire. It's the last of my long weekend before I go to work again. I've oiled and sharpened my shears and filed new edges on my shovels. My own yard is not a good reference.

Mrs. Amanda Wilson (another friend of Alice's) has a yard the size of mine that I care for once a week. There are no spiders in her tree crotches. I wave them away, into corners. She sits at a white wrought-iron table on the terrace and watches me. She has her tea and her newspaper, but they are only props. She was raised to be on her guard around people like me.

When I was there the other day, mowing, her grandchildren were visiting. They ran after me, in the wake of the lawnmower, kicking up the freshly cut grass and staining the bottoms of their brown feet. They fenced with pruned limbs from the pear tree. They ran their hands through the earth, looking for weeds I may have missed.

They asked questions, as children do. Children have only two needs: to know and to help.

"How do you know what a weed is?" one of them asked me.

"A weed looks less orderly," I told them. "Less purposeful." That was a lie. I said it because Mrs. Amanda Wilson was listening, and it was the kind of thing she'd like to hear from her gardener. I felt bad about telling them that—children, at least, deserve the truth—but I didn't correct it.

"How do you know which branches to cut off?"

That was a good question, too. "A good gardener can tell the ones that won't bear fruit." Another lie.

"How?"

"By the number of leaves on it. By the way it bends in the hand. By the feel of its bark."

"Why do you mow the grass?"

"Doesn't it smell good?"

"Yes." "Yes."

"That's why." Lies, lies.

Mrs. Amanda Wilson called them inside, then, so they wouldn't bother me.

The spider has found her way onto the rim of the coffee cup, circling the dark, cold liquid as only spiders can, eight steps at a time. I shake her off into the grass.

Alice is back, calling from the porch. "Tony?"

I stare at the barbecue, thinking of the children, and I ignore her. This is new to me, being intentionally rude.

"Tony? Yoo-hoo, Tony?"

I imagine, with failing peripheral vision, her hesitancy (Is he deaf, now, too?): one step down onto the lawn, and then backing up the step to the porch again, and finally, defeated, turning to go. "I'll come back later," she says. "At a better time."

"It's all right, Alice. Come ahead." But it won't accomplish anything; money won't solve Alice's problems, and it won't solve mine. She seems to think that life is a game show.

"I've found a darling house for you, with a large yard," she says.

"For God's sake, Alice, you can't market everything. The world isn't for sale."

"Of course you can." She is genuinely surprised. "Of course it is. What makes you believe the things you do?" She gives me that odd gesture with one hand that says, *Silly.*

"I'm happy, Alice. Happy. Happy. Happy, damn it." I leer at her with what I take to be a foolish, contented grin, but what is probably something else entirely in her eyes. (Lunatic. Drooling, near-blind idiot.) I've heard her, talking to others, call me "that mourning, mournful man." I am. I admit it.

She may be right, after all. Life may be a game show.

At sunset, after she's gone, the coals are nearly done in their white heat. The spider has moved to the wall, where her shadow was this morning. The cat is back at my feet, dreaming.

The sun, now from the wrong direction, catches the spider again, and a swallow hits the wall in a swimmer's turn, takes it, and is gone.

THE LAST AMERICAN
LIVING IN CUBA

When Prophet finds a level place, he sits on his heels and pinches the handkerchief he has carried from home into a parachute. He wipes his forehead and his ears and the back of his neck and then carefully folds it again into a diamond shape before running it twice around the leather inside his white Panama hat. He puts the handkerchief back in his left breast pocket. He squares the hat over his eyes and watches.

Small girls in black dresses are shadows on a bright dance floor. *Da-da-da-rum-dum, da-da-da-rum-dum.* There's a hitch in the music, a drummer's soft brushes: *da-da-da-rum-dum, ssssst, da-da-da-rum-dum.* It slips in underneath like a snake skidding on pavement.

Soft red and green lights hang suspended in the tops of old magnolias, and Prophet (as if from a height) can see in his imagination Havana's once-palatial homes bisected by white sunlight and purple shade. The terminator is a scratch of lavender smoke across red tile roofs. He wants to stand and stretch. He wants to snap his fingers in time and push his hat back in a friendly way and go down and dance. If it weren't raining, if he wouldn't have to fight for every muddy step through twisted hanging roots, he thinks that would be exactly the thing to do.

But it *is* raining, rattling like gravel in the hard, flat leaves above his head and running down the trunks in oily beads. When he reaches out to touch it, it is hot.

The music loses its tempo and almost stops, then quickens into a tango. The tango turns into a foxtrot, and the dancers meet and slow and whirl, the girls' black dresses spreading open like umbrellas. The smell of cinnamon rises from the earth. It must have been like this in Cuba before the Revolution, in Cuba when he was young, before he had to go alone to live with an uncle in Miami.

The band dissolves in a burst of fireworks that scatters the dancers. They stop under the trees and stand singly or in pairs to watch. The *crump* of each exploding shell taps against the bones in his ear. Their showers make red triangles of his hands.

"Tango foxtrot, damn it."

The music he hears *da-rum-dum* is his heart beating, the rain falling, and *ssssst,* Prophet tells himself to be quiet.

"Go, now."

Words from a language Prophet doesn't know fly through the air like insects. *Geaunau.*

"Now! Now!"

He lets the sound roll through him, giving it no more of his attention than to think that it might be a chant, a spell, a hoo-doo rite; something strangely Haitian washed up on these shores.

"Go!"

The trees around him are splitting. It's the lightning, he thinks. Tree-hearts crouch out crablike into the open. They walk sideways, doubled over; dark, humped stumps carrying weapons slide down into the clearing.

"Prophet!" He hears *Profit.* What bargain was struck? what trade consummated?

The dancers are stumbling over their own feet, falling like firewood. He is as confused as they.

There is still Bangkok, for dancing and light. There will always be Beirut. But Saigon is (sigh) gone, and Havana no longer likes parties. Santiago is slowly poisoning itself. Prophet goes to Rio.

From his stone balcony, Prophet can look down at the ships and small craft that float on the greasy water like wreckage. A huge Christ stands over the harbor, too, welcoming the tired, the poor, and those who, like Prophet, have been tossed onto Brazil's teeming shore. Liberty stood like this when he first saw her, when he and his five sisters were forced to flee Havana for New York.

The long white beaches are littered with half-naked, large-breasted women who lie in the sun like crucifixes. Prophet walks carefully among these saints, stepping cautiously even though his feet are burning. His work is to lift their hands and feet and check their palms and ankles for holes.

Here's one. There's another. He stoops to inspect a sweating brown back and its purple birthmark. He brushes away beads of oil that have collected on her spine and sees that it is a tattoo in the shape of France. Dark wine colors have seeped into the sand underneath her.

He straightens and looks at all the work he has left to do. The girls stretch in brown humps and black bikinied bottoms nearly to the horizon. He wants to pull their legs together; he wants to fold their arms across their sagging breasts.

Up the beach in the hotels, roulette wheels are spinning. The pea-sized ball rattles and bounces and drops. Twenty-nine, black and odd.

"Twenty-nine."

"Bring the evidence. Need a knife?"

Prophet steps out of the shadows. Green tables sit in cones of yellow light. The backs of cards glow like shards of phosphorescence, are spun out, picked up, turned over. Dice roll, stop, and stare back at him emptily. The roulette layout is a map, a grid of squares on green felt. He bets all his money on his birth date and wins.

The woman sitting next to him half turns to smile. She has a new sunburn, and he can feel her heat. Light strikes the sequins of her dress and she glitters like a rainbow rising to take a lure. She shines like a mirrored chandelier. When he looks over the tops of her bare shoulders into the dark crevice between her breasts, he sees a ruby as big as an eyeball on a braided chain glowing with its own red fire. He bets on red and wins again.

Prophet gambles until he's won the bank. He's a bit surprised at how easy it is. The casino's lights flicker and then brighten. He shades his eyes. The dealers look at him reproachfully and stop the wheels with a hand and sheathe their tables in slick, black plastic bags.

"Take it easy."

Prophet and his little brother fly out in a Piper Cub with two strangers when they escape Havana. He rubs his brother's head to reassure him as the plane pitches and rolls. His brother's hair is hot and greasy under his hand. He tries to answer the questions about where they're going—New Orleans—but he has to make most of it up.

New Orleans is a fine town; if he'd been asked, he couldn't have designed a better one. Bartenders at back doors smuggle out to them sagging plates of rice and shrimp and hand the boys bottles of Jax beer still icy with fingerprints. The prostitutes let them sleep next to them in warm, perfumed beds. Prophet lies naked on his back against Carmen or Maria in the sweet-smelling time before dawn, counting the slow revolutions the propeller of her ceiling fan makes as it spins lazily, or he turns into her and puts a hand on her breast, liking the feel of it and the feel of her alive inside it. Rain on the tiles of the balcony smears the neon into puddles, and the tangle of red hair on the pillow silk smells of cinnamon.

There is no escaping this. The two dead are zipped up and stacked on top of each other and everybody knows this one will die too before they get back. Prophet's Panama has disappeared to somewhere, blown off or sucked out or just lost. The helicopter slips sideways, barely clearing the trees, and Prophet sits with his back to the open door and holds the wounded man the way he would his wife, stroking his bare, white chest in meaningless circles. Maybe to lift the pain out. The heart beating under his hand belongs to the medic.

The lieutenant is shouting something to Prophet, but Prophet can't make out the words over the beat of the rotors. He nods to the lieutenant anyway, and that is enough, apparently: the lieutenant turns to shout at somebody else.

Nice shimmers in the heat of an Indian summer.

On the drive down from San Remo through Monaco and into France, the narrow road turns Prophet again and again into the sheetmetal-bright Mediterranean, until he has to close his eyes on the corners against its glare. A horn freezes him for a second, but then he reacts and manages to squeeze between a poultry truck and a tiny red motorcycle, and then in two more turnings he sees the city tumbling down the hills in white blocks to the sea.

In Nice he rests under umbrella shade at a thin metal table, though the road seems to be unwinding underneath him still and his hands won't stop shaking from his near miss with the motorcycle. The drink he grips is clear and oily, and he guesses it is ouzo. The sidewalk is crowded with shoppers stepping through leaf shadows. He smiles at the blonde-haired girls who have wrapped themselves in tight, short skirts like bright packages, who are gifts to the world, and they smile back. They pull their hair back for a moment into hand-held ponytails and saunter down the boulevard, and he thinks the loveliest sight on earth must be tanned legs ending in high heels.

The waiter brings him another drink, although he hasn't yet finished his first or asked for another. He lifts out a coffee bean with his fingernail and places it on his tongue. It's anisette he's drinking.

He shouldn't be here, drinking this. Where is the wine that his family shared on the veranda? What of the dances, the whole family—brothers and sisters, aunts and uncles—arm in arm? What has become of his mother's crystal: those fine globes on top of tall stems half-full of purple? He smiles at the memory of dipping his hands into them, staining his fingertips. Where is the blue cloud from good cigars? (His father would light one, sighing, and say it was better than sex. His mother, horrified, a finger to her lips, would whisper, "*Ssssst.*") Where are the cool breezes, the evening's long colors? Where is the noise of frogs and night birds? What has happened? He even misses the bite and whine of mosquitoes. What has happened? What has happened? The tongue-sharp smell of sugarcane is gone.

He tastes oil, blown back through the breather. His hands are slick. The medic on his lap is dead when they bank around to land.

"Go, now."

Blue and red smoke crawls across the ground beneath them and then is caught in the wind—*da-rum-dum*—of the rotors. Prophet wipes his own face with his handkerchief and then the dead man's girlish features, smoothing the lines around his eyes. He sees a purpose in his actions, after all: the blood on the medic's chest has been smeared into a bull's-eye.

PLAYING OUT OF THE
DEEP WOODS

If it's the second week in September at the Hollow Hills Country Club, it's the annual Married Couples Best Ball Tournament. It started as fun, as these things do, but over the years it has grown the thick skin of tradition and the cement-hard weight of competition and bad feelings, and at times the practice rounds have led to hatred and divorce. Not so this year. This year the greens committee has decreed that trophies will go to all contestants, that first prize will be a dozen new balls and a free dinner instead of a new set of Ping irons, and that the old tricks of *longest drive, closest to the pin,* and *best sand save* will regain their old importance. This year, they decreed, it will be fun again.

Even so, every tournament has pressure. Particularly if the wife is an eight handicap and the husband a thirteen (like the Nylans), or, worse, if husband and wife are completely mismatched (like the Hollisters).

Teddy Nylan was a thirteen. His wife, Jo, could give him a run for his money from the blue blocks. Her three iron alone brought tears to his eyes. "She knocks it a hundred and eighty yards," he liked to tell men, "and she can stop it in a foot and a half." And she could, too. Her putts never bounced. She never shanked a short iron. He admired her game with the generosity of heart of a man still in love with his wife after half a lifetime of marriage and with the respect one good golfer owes another.

Jo Nylan was one of those fierce little Texas blondes who could drink men stupid and then drive them home, weighed always 102 pounds, and looked to be forever 26 years old. She was funny, bright, beautiful, and devastatingly accurate inside 150 yards. She called the small bushes that served as yardage markers "my trees."

"How'd you end up?" Teddy would ask as they got near her shot. "A club back from my tree," she would tell him.

Teddy was her perfect match. A native Texan, too, he was tall, large, and slow-moving, with a deep appreciation for fun and a possessive pride in his diminutive partner. They loved to team up and pull some of the old Lee Trevino sucker bets on their opponents, waiting, for instance, for Jo to play some tough par four beautifully, leaving herself eleven feet from the pin in two, and when the expected appreciation for her shot would come from a member of the foursome, Teddy would drawl, "Ah, that's *luck.* She cain't par it."

"What do you mean, I can't par it?" Jo would say.

"Yeah," the sucker would pipe up, smitten by her beauty and her shot.

Teddy would wink at the mark and say, in a whisper, "She three-putts something awful under pressure."

"You're making me mad, Teddy."

"I say you cain't par it."

And so the bet would happen—greens fees all around and a dozen balls or new head covers and then dinner at the club afterward—and Jo would step up and almost negligently sink the putt for birdie.

"See, there," the sucker would say, and hug Jo.

"Yep," Teddy would say slowly, "but it ain't *par.*"

They were a match.

So much so that Teddy would have a handicap lower than his wife's if he could only solve that wild slice that would sometimes show up unexpectedly, like in-laws. He'd have a real chance of shooting a 75, and then the slice would come and he'd find himself out-of-bounds or in a hazard or in deep woods that he'd insist on playing out of.

Jo loved this wild side of him, for all the damage it did to his game. It reminded her of the way he'd been as a young man, buying a bottle of champagne on a whim and packing a suitcase (with none of the right things) and spiriting her off to a sudden weekend in Arkansas or Mexico. He'd buy her flowers or coats or jewelry at the drop of a hat and worry about how to pay for it all later. She loved that part of her husband, and if it showed up once in a while in him as a wicked slice, she would live with that.

Teddy wouldn't. Teddy, for all his climate-slow talking and funeral-paced stride, was possessed by a mercurial temper that always surprised him. He got his tantrums, he'd say, the way other men got sneezes: in a series of quick, powerful blows that arose from the depths in him without warning. Jo would scurry out of the way of it, having learned years ago not to try to joke him out of his anger, but Teddy, of course, with no place to hide, had to go the distance. And when his Maxfli took that soft, slow turn to the right and headed for the trees, for a hazard, for another county, Teddy would lift his offending driver above his head and bend it into the same shape as his ball's flight and then hurl it into those same trees or that same hazard.

Jo had quit counting the cost, though he averaged a new driver every month or so. And there was no guarantee that the three wood wouldn't desert him, or the two iron either. More than once he'd finished a round with only a nine, three wedges, and his putter. At moments like these, Jo held onto the fact that he *finished the round.* Teddy Nylan was not one to quit.

The Nylans were favorites going into this year's Married Couples Best Ball Tournament at Hollow Hills, but close behind were the Hollisters. Howard Hollister had a better handicap than either of the Nylans—plus one—but his wife, Margerie, had never shot better than 140 in her life. That the Hollisters remained married was a mystery to the other members. Though Margerie loved the game—and worked at it—she never understood its fundamentals (getting her hips through, for one), and she could no longer cajole her husband into helping. (He'd tried once, a decade or two ago, the story went, but had nearly killed her in a rage with her own clubs when she duffed the ball fourteen times in a row and then put two in the water and took a 37 on an easy par four.)

As these things go, because God *does* like to fool with us—and likes to fool with golfers most of all—the Nylans and the Hollisters were paired by lot into a foursome for the tournament and given an early tee time.

Margerie, frankly, in a best ball tournament, was along for the ride. She'd sometimes, out of luck, sink a putt her husband missed, but that was all, and if she helped win that one hole in eighteen she'd done her job. Howard, giving a stroke back to par, made no mistakes. No duck hook or slice lurked in his game. He birdied few holes, but bogeyed even fewer. From the tee, Howard would see the safest spot to land his ball, and then he'd land it there. He honestly didn't know why everybody didn't do the same. When his wife lunged wildly and sent the ball skittering forty yards, he'd turn his eyes to heaven not in exasperation but for explanation. Why? he'd ask, not comprehending, and the answer he'd always get would be the enigmatic one God had given Job: *Because.*

That second Sunday in September the four of them stood on the 1st tee at the compass points, and Howard flipped a tee into the air, one that landed and pointed to Margerie. He tossed it again: Teddy. He tossed it a third time: himself.

"Okay, honey," he said to his wife. "Swing easy."

She didn't. She leapt at the ball as if it were a drowning child, and Fate, not waiting to conspire, slowed her hands enough that she connected, and to everybody's surprise the ball lifted as if it had a tailwind and traveled two hundred yards before it faded lazily and ended up in the trees.

"'Shot," he said to her, amazed. "Best you've ever hit."

"I'm sorry it's in the trees," she said, not sorry at all, happier than she'd ever been with a club in her hand. "I won't be much help to you."

"But it's in the trees *a long way* out," he said, and gave her a hug.

Teddy congratulated her, too, and teed up his ball. He knew Hollister was the trouble for them in this tournament, but he knew if he could keep his slice locked up he and Jo stood a good chance. *Draw* was his swing thought, but the result was a 300-yard blast that nearly took the top off a live oak as it dived into the trees.

Teddy bent his driver and shoved the pretzel back into his bag for later.

The 1st hole—and maybe the tournament—had come down already to the best two golfers. Casey in Mudville hadn't more confidence than Howard as he stepped up for his first drive of the day.

"He never misses," Margerie told Jo. "He hasn't had to take a mulligan since he was twelve. He says he's saved them all these years for me."

Jo nodded. She'd seen him play and knew his mechanics to be beyond reproach. In fact, it was no secret that Howard wanted to play a round a day for the next nine years and then try for the Senior Tour. If he could develop some dazzle, he thought, some *imagination,* he'd match himself against touring pros at the end of their careers.

The crack of club meeting ball seemed to suck with it the air, and in the vacuum left behind on the tee four pairs of eyes watched in astonishment as the ball rose straight and true as if climbing stairs, gathering itself higher and higher until, at the zenith of its arc, it turned hard right into the deep woods.

"I don't slice," he said, in the same way he'd say to a homicide detective, "I don't murder children."

"You do now," Teddy said.

"I wouldn't call that a slice," Jo said. "I'm not sure what it was, but it wasn't a slice."

"Maybe a UFO," Margerie said.

"We'll concede the hole," Howard said.

"You can't do that," Jo said. "Besides, it would take the fun out of it." She pulled out her driver.

"Hit your three iron," Teddy told her, suddenly superstitious. "You hit such a beautiful three."

She thanked him for that, but swung her driver anyway, and she caught the ball with the toe of her club—or she didn't; it didn't seem to matter—and the ball soared into the woods with the others.

"What balls are y'all playing?" Teddy asked. "I've got a Maxfli 2."

"Ultra 1," Jo said.

"Titleist," Howard said. "I don't remember the number." As he hadn't lost a ball in fifteen years, he never remembered their numbers.

"All I know about mine," Margerie said, "is it's pink."

"Let's go."

"Let's all just take another off the tee," Margerie said. "Mulligans. It's all the same."

Howard looked an apology to Jo and Teddy, and another one to his wife, and still another to God. "That's not golf," he said.

So they walked to the woods.

The right side of the 1st hole at Hollow Hills is live oak and pine and sycamore and, forty yards in, a gulley that winds down into a darkness so complete it's romantic. No balls had ever been recovered from that darkness; not even the caddies, who collected lost balls (and sometimes stole them from the men they caddied for) and sold them back to the pro shop, dared go down there. Teddy was in the woods only a few minutes before he realized he'd need a flashlight.

The first one to go in was Margerie. The woods swallowed her in an instant, and Howard felt a momentary pang in his heart as if he'd watched her drop over the side of their sloop and sink like a weight.

"Okay in there?" he called, embarrassed that he had.

"Okay," she called back, but she sounded far off.

Jo was next. She went in bravely, waving to her husband.

The men stood together for a moment, in the light of the fairway, judging where their balls had gone in.

"I'm a little in front of you, I think," Teddy said.

"Maybe twenty yards," Howard agreed.

"'Bout here, I think."

"Looks right," Howard said.

"Well, see you."

"See you."

And Howard was left alone.

Howard, still stunned that he'd have to go into the woods at all, stood at the tree line as if facing a problem without solution. What do you do? he wondered. Just lift up a branch and go in? And then what? He considered cheating—but only for an instant; no, less than an instant—by dropping another ball just inside the trees and claiming it had struck a trunk and bounced back, but to his credit he dismissed the thought before he realized that *none* of the shots had hit solidly against trees, and that seemed odd. He'd heard enough of Margerie's hit trees, and those of partners he didn't play with twice; they do *thonk,* he thought. These hadn't.

He felt the sunlight on his arms and the back of his neck like a mother's hand, and then, waving the foursome behind on through, he parted the branches and stepped into the trees.

Margerie found her pink Flying Lady almost at once. It had done what her husband's hadn't, and had been flicked back near the fairway. With a low, hard long iron, she might be able to play it where it lay. She stepped back out for advice just in time to see her husband go in, so in a thoughtful daze she went back in, too. Behind her pink ball she saw a yellow glimmer, and behind that a white one, and then another, and then an orange one, and so, like one of the kids in the fairy tale following a trail of bread crumbs, she picked up one ball after another and worked her way further into the trees. After all the balls she'd lost, she was owed this.

Jo had a harder time and discovered a different treasure.

She poked about with her three iron for five minutes before it struck something, and when she bent down to see what, she found a locket. It wasn't a cheap dime-store locket that some giggler might have lost while thrashing about with her boyfriend, but a good, gold one, one like her mother had worn on a delicately braided, rose-colored chain. With lightness of heart, she opened it, and stared at a picture of herself.

Teddy flung his twisted driver up into a crotch as soon as he was out of sight. He knew the ball was in deep, but he'd give it the required five minutes before he took a drop. They all should have taken a stroke-and-distance penalty from the tee, and it bothered him that they hadn't. *Why* hadn't they? Margerie's suggestion of mulligans, he thought. Second chances. The superstition he'd felt before Jo teed off now darkened into a real worry. He rose up and bumped his head.

Howard was already lost. He hadn't taken two steps into the trees before he became disoriented. What purpose did this have on a golf course? A golf course was a mown lawn and a flag. The trees on the sides had always been scenery to him. In a sudden panic he turned around three times and rushed into the ravine.

Margie had an armload. The brightly colored balls seemed to glow with their own light in this dark place. She'd taken up the game because Howard loved it so, but to be truthful it was the bright colors that she found most interesting. Here they all were—the sunlight, the course, the clothes—compressed into dimpled spheres. She thought vaguely of an image that she couldn't express—even to herself, but it was this: tiny suns containing the potential of their own planets.

When they spilled from her forearms and elbow crotches, she shrugged out of her top and belted its sleeves around the V-neck and had a knit sack. Her brassiere glowed like a white shirt under black light.

Jo hung the locket around her neck and thought of her mother. She accepted this gift calmly and could only assume that the ghost of her mother had placed it here for her, and she was certain that her very calmness was proof of an afterlife.

She swung her three iron easily—almost idly—but purposefully, the way women since the beginning of time have swung scythes, rocked babies, planted seeds, in a dreamless repetition of motion that is pattern, rhythm. It struck metal again and the clank sent a shock up her wrist and into her shoulder. She knew before she bent down and looked that she would find a tiny pair of bronzed shoes.

Had Teddy known of his wife's peace, he might have been less frightened, but the knock he'd taken served to exaggerate the danger he already felt. He tried to calm himself. He stood, ducking a little out of reflex, and pictured the sunlit fairway only steps in one direction or another. He knew that it ran north-to-south, and he remembered that moss grew on the north sides of trees, so he looked up into the branches and was surprised to see, dangling like Dali's clocks, limp drivers and long irons and three woods.

The air went out of him and he sank to his knees in the damp humus and began to sob. He had never in his life sobbed.

Howard ran into dark and then darker darkness, as if he were being drawn like a needle to North. A word escaped him like a wail, though he didn't know it, and it carried through the woods, banging from limb to limb like a blind bird.

He ran downhill, knowing as he did that it was wrong.

When Margie had filled her blouse with pretty balls, she pulled off her white slacks and knotted each leg and filled that new, double sack.

Now clothes hung from the branches, clothes she had worn as a child and as a young woman, clothes she had for years carefully draped on hangers and stowed in her closets and then in the attic. She brushed her hand across them again lovingly, recapturing their colors and scents.

Stockings dangled. She found underwear and shoes in heaps. Margie walked in a part of the woods that hid citrus trees, and the roof above her opened so that sunlight glittered on oranges, lemons, and they gleamed. She reached to crush a dark, waxy leaf and grasped, instead, the invisibility of a favorite article of lingerie. What had become of that? She unhooked her brassiere and dropped it coyly like a lace handkerchief. She bent to touch her toes and pulled her pink cotton briefs down at the same time, and then worked them roughly over the spikes of her shoes.

Jo was sobbing nearly as hard as her husband, but Jo sobbed for joy. Had she listened carefully, she might even have heard him—he was only fifty yards away—but of course people sobbing, for joy or otherwise, hear only what they wish.

Jo's dead mother sat on a low branch, her knees drawn up to her chest in the way she'd sat in Jo's earliest memories, with her back supported by a hand of air. She was rocking, slowly, and smiling languidly in her daughter's direction, and humming the lullaby that Jo recognized with some part of her other than memory.

"I want a daughter, too," Jo said, and her mother nodded and hummed.

It wouldn't be Teddy's. Teddy wanted children as badly as Jo, and had since he was young, but in twenty years of marriage they'd never been given so much as a false alarm; Jo had never been more than a day late.

They'd never discussed the problem—only the desire—but Teddy, because he had to know, had made an appointment at one of those fertility clinics on the sly, and had taken a morning from work. They'd closeted him with a pornographic film and a specimen bottle and told him to let nature do the work, but he'd had to sit through the short movie three times before he could put aside his disgust long enough to do what had to be done.

They called him back three days later with the results.

"They're too slow," the doctor told him.

"They are?"

"*Real* slow. They don't hardly move at all."

"They don't?"

The doctor shook his head. "We can inseminate your wife with your sperm, Mr. Nylan; we help them along a little, get them started."

"Help them along?"

"Get them started."

Teddy understood then that the doctor wanted to *place* his spermatozoa in Jo's womb, to save them the trip, so to speak, and he imagined chairs with stirrups and eye-searing fluorescent lights and gloved fingers and glass tubes and stainless-steel instruments, and he refused.

He never talked to Jo about any of this; he never talked to anyone, he just refused.

It occurred to Howard that perhaps the absolute darkness of the place he was in had something to do with him, with his golf, with his life. As if he weren't frightened enough.

His life—and his golf game—had no stray ends, and never had. He'd been a machine inside a machine, ordered, perfect, but now the wail escaped him again and rose up into the branches again and he heard the *thwock* of it strike each tree like the balls he'd never given up.

When he got deep into the ravine, he reached a level place and stopped.

Their mechanical lovemaking had always hurt Margie. Emotionally, and—something inside—spiritually, and physically. She'd watched him on the driving range, pounding ball after ball into the 250-yard target. Lovemaking was like that. Pause, *whack*. Pause, *whack*. Pause, *whack*.

She'd taken the blame for it, until now.

She stood in a short circle of light under an orange tree and looked down at herself, taking inspection as everybody does from time to time. She was slim—no, skinny—and seemed even more so, naked in golf shoes. She did not have pretty legs, but they were firm. Her breasts were small. Her nipples were the size of collar buttons. She was plain, in every regard. But she was honest and true and generous, and damn it, she wasn't a golf ball for her husband to tee up and drive.

When her mother climbed down from the limb, Jo followed her into the ravine without comment or complaint. A hum filled the air now (it was Howard's). It seemed to be in front of her: a keening noise, almost a complaint, or perhaps a desire.

She began to run, wanting more than anything to be coupled with that sound, and that the sound took on a shape and substance and that the shape of it was a man and its substance was hard seemed perfectly all right. She clawed at him, toppling him, and then she sat astride him, and not once did the *him* matter. He was in all respects a tool and she in all respects a void, and soundlessly—except for that weird keening that rushed through the trees like a wind—they performed together the first act and the last act and the only act, and brought substance out of chaos.

Teddy felt a tug in his solar plexus that passed, and then a relief that didn't, and he knew his tantrums were gone forever. Once his fear vanished, he got his bearings and gave up his ball as lost and walked without hesitation to the fairway.

Jo joined him in fifteen minutes, smiling, and cupped one of his large hands in both of hers. How she loved him! How it showed!

Margerie struggled out nearly half an hour later, not far from where the Nylans stood in love. She clutched a diaphanous pink veil to her skinny waist and smiled at them shyly. Neither Teddy nor Jo gave any sign that she was a strange sight, naked, in golf shoes, on the 1st fairway of Hollow Hills.

"My wedding night," she said to Jo.

"Mine, too," Jo said.

"It's lovely," said Teddy, meaning the teddy.

The three of them stood there as the tournament went on without them, and they waited until dark at the edge of the fairway, but Howard never came back out.

THE
PRACTICE COURT-MARTIAL
OF PRIVATE PETERSON

Everyone knew it was Peterson who shot the General's dog; Peterson, it was pointed out, had sworn to kill Ludwig, and Peterson, it was agreed, was, although a little weird, a man of his word. Scuttlebutt had it that he'd climbed up into a low tree behind the PX and whistled the recognition signal, the General's low warble, and then drilled the beast right between his brown beady eyes when he skidded around the corner. General Hilling launched an inquiry with his usual efficiency—*Who shot my dog? Peterson, sir. Hang him.*—and didn't concern himself with the details.

The details fell to an old major named Mayse at the end of his career. Had someone other than Mayse been appointed Investigating Officer, they might have hung Peterson after all, but Mayse, a ground-pounding private at Guadalcanal and Okinawa and a young lieutenant at Inchon, knew all about long hot evenings and rear-area boredom and generals and generals' dogs. That's to say he had all the sympathy in the world for Peterson and a bone-tired disgust of the wreckage of war. So he called Peterson into his office, which was one desk and one chair tucked into the corner of a Quonset hut crammed with blankets no one wanted, and asked him to stand at ease. A small, wall-mounted fan ticked apologetically and breathed warm air. Major Mayse pushed his knuckles into his eyes and then leaned on his elbows.

"Did you shoot the General's dog, Peterson?"

"No, sir."

"Well, I had to ask."

Mayse tipped his chair back until it settled against the wall. He put his feet up on the open upper-left-hand desk drawer and tugged on his nose. He looked Peterson over carefully.

Peterson looked like any other Marine. One hand rested on the barrel of his rifle, which leaned against his leg, and one hand was out of sight behind his back. He was tall, skinny, young, dark-eyed, and had the beginnings of a smile that didn't know which way to go. He had the smug look of a combat Marine who hadn't yet seen any combat. Or maybe, Mayse reminded himself, it was the look of someone who had shot the General's dog. He saw a lot of smug looks in the rear-area. Some were scared, and some weren't, but once in the bush it didn't seem to matter either way.

"Are you any good with that rifle, son?"

"I can shoot it."

Mayse let his weight slide forward. His boots hit the floor with flat heels at the same moment he slapped the desk with his palms. Peterson jumped.

"That's not what I asked. I asked if you're any good with it."

"Yes, sir. Expert."

"What kind of shooting do you suppose it would take to put one hole between the eyes of a Doberman on a dead run?"

"Good shooting, sir," Peterson said.

"Good shooting?"

"Expert shooting, sir."

Major Mayse sighed. "Middle of the night, it would take a lot of luck, too, don't you think?"

"Yes, sir."

"Good luck or bad luck, I don't know. But luck." He tugged on his nose again and caught himself doing it. He brought his hand down with an effort. "I'm going to lay this out straight, Peterson. You look real good for this, and the General wants a body for his dog's. I'm going to have one hell of a time giving him one, though, because no one saw the little kraut get zapped. And that leaves you in a funny position." Mayse saw something like interest creep into Peterson's eyes. It would be fear, Mayse thought, if the boy had any sense.

"You're all alone on a hill, Peterson. On your right flank, someone says he saw you shoot the General's dog. You get court-martialed and sent home, or at the very least you do some safe time in the brig. On your left flank, if I know my commanding generals—and I do—there are orders sending you into the bush tomorrow at oh-dark-thirty." Mayse paused to let it sink in. "You see what I'm driving at, don't you?"

"I think I do, sir. Yes, sir," Peterson said.

"Did you shoot the General's dog, Peterson?"

"No, sir."

"How come?"

"What's that?"

"Never mind. Get out of here."

"Aye, aye, sir."

"Yeah." Mayse waved him out and reached for his nose.

That should have been the end of it—it was, as far as Mayse was concerned—but later that afternoon General Hilling sent Major Mayse another major and said to get on with it.

"Get on with what?" Mayse wanted to know.

"With the trial," Major Sullivan said. Sullivan was a short, redheaded Irishman cursed with a toothy grin and a tic that pulled his left eye down into a lascivious wink whenever he was excited. When the smile and tic were working together—as they were now—he looked demented. "The General thinks we should take a run at it. You know, a practice court-martial. See how things go."

"A *practice* court-martial?"

"That's it," Sullivan said, leering. "That's the General's ticket. Just to see how things go. If they go good, we'll chopper in some legal beagles and do it for real."

"There isn't any evidence," Mayse said.

"Ah." Sullivan walked to the door and turned to stab at Mayse with a finger. "Evidence." He waited a minute and then said, a little louder, "Evidence!"

A pair of MPs carried in a stiff-legged Doberman and laid him on the floor. The Investigating Officer looked down at the dog—its tongue lolling, its hindquarters askew, a small neat hole in its forehead—and then looked up at Sullivan. "That's a dead dog," he told him.

"Right," Sullivan said, and grinned. "This is Ludwig. Exhibit 1."

Mayse bowed his head and covered his eyes.

"Ludwig," Sullivan continued, "was with malice aforethought lured into a trap fiendishly devised and then brutally—"

"Major Sullivan."

Sullivan blinked. "Brutally—"

"I'm not a jury," Mayse said.

"No, Major," Major Sullivan said, "you're the trial counsel."

"The what?"

"The prosecuting attorney in this case."

"I'm the Investigating Officer," Mayse said. "And I've investigated. There is no case."

"The General says there is," Sullivan said, "and you're to present it."

"And what will you do?"

"I'm the defense counsel," Sullivan said glumly.

"Trade you."

"I've already tried. The General wants you to prosecute." He gave Mayse a look that said it wasn't fair.

Mayse got up and stood over Ludwig. "Then this is my exhibit?"

Sullivan nodded.

Mayse toed the corpse. "Get it out of here," he told the MPs.

"Hold on," Sullivan said.

"Bury it," said Mayse.

"That's physical evidence!"

"It certainly is," Mayse said. "And it's starting to turn. Bury it." He held up a hand to ward off Sullivan's objection. "We can stipulate to the dead dog in court," he said. "Under oath."

"Well, then." Sullivan showed his teeth. "That's fine."

When the MPs had dragged Ludwig out, Mayse looked for a long time at the stain the dog had left, and then up to Sullivan. "Did you really think that a court-martial board would demand—or even desire—to see the Doberman?"

"It's evidence," Sullivan said. He was sulking. "What other evidence is there?"

"My point," Mayse said. "There isn't any."

"I had to dig him up and hose him off," Sullivan said softly. He was talking to himself, so Mayse didn't interrupt. "What about justice?"

"What about it?" Mayse asked.

"What about the General, then?"

Yeah, Mayse thought, what about that? If he wasn't careful, he'd end up in the bush with Peterson. He was too old for that crap. He knew—having had a vision—that the next time in the bush would be his last. "Who's serving as judge?" he asked, scared of the answer.

"Armbruster," Sullivan said.

"Armbruster?" Who was Armbruster? The new motor pool officer? The General's aide?

"Sergeant Armbruster."

"The *cook*?"

Sullivan nodded. "That one."

"Arm-bruiser," Major Mayse said, and sat back in his chair. "Arm-bruiser, the cook, staff judge advocate in a court-martial proceeding." He shook his head.

"Practice judge," Sullivan corrected him, "in a practice court-martial."

"Do you know him?" Mayse demanded.

"I've seen him around," Sullivan said evasively.

"He's goofy." Mayse tapped his temple twice. "Isn't right." He tapped it again. "Hasn't got," he said, spacing his words, "a full seabag."

"Maybe that's why the General picked him," Sullivan said, and after that there wasn't anything more to say.

The General, in an effort to be fair, gave Peterson a week to prepare his defense. Peterson came to see Major Mayse.

"I like you, son," Mayse said to the young Marine standing at attention, "but you have appointed counsel. Major Sullivan. Go see him."

"He scares me," Peterson said.

"I don't blame you. But he's preparing your side of things."

"He's out of town, sir."

"We're in the middle of the goddamn jungle. How can he be out of town?"

"He's in Saigon, sir."

"Doing what?"

"He didn't tell me. Look, sir, I want a lawyer."

"I don't blame you for that, either. If this thing goes to a trial, you'll get one. Sit down, Peterson."

Peterson looked around and pulled a stack of blankets over in front of the Major's desk and sat on them.

When Peterson had stopped swaying and was balanced, Mayse said, "The General, in his own way, is giving you a good defense. He's made me prosecutor. And I don't think this case can be prosecuted. I've been looking through the Articles, and—"

"Articles?"

"The Articles of the Uniform Code of Military Justice, Peterson. We have to charge you with one of them, and there's nothing in here about dog-shooting." Mayse held up a thick, maroon, loose-leaf binder with gold letters. "I'm going to have to bend one or two to fit. You want to help me decide which?"

"Sure. I guess. Sir."

"Okay," Mayse said, pulling the notebook open to a place he had marked. "There's Article 80, *attempts*. As I see it, I'd have to prove you were *attempting* something else by shooting the General's dog."

"Such as what?"

"I don't know. Something illegal."

Peterson thought for a moment and then said, "What else have you got?"

"Article 88, *contempt,*" Mayse said.

"Contempt for Ludwig?"

"All right, Article 89, *disrespect to a superior officer.* Shooting Ludwig could be considered disrespectful to the General."

"I suppose so," Peterson said.

"Article 90," Mayse said, turning the page. *"Assault and/or willful disobedience."*

"No one said *not* to shoot the dog," Peterson said. It was as close as Peterson had come to admitting guilt, and Mayse ignored it.

"Article 93, *cruelty, maltreatment.* That's probably what I'll end up with. One 5.56-millimeter round in the dog's brain housing. That's cruelty, Peterson. That's maltreatment."

Peterson nodded.

"Did you like the dog?"

"What's that, sir?"

"Did you like the dog?"

Peterson smelled a trap. "Like him, sir?"

"Well, for instance, if your defense counsel is going to show a personal and intense mutual dislike for each other, I could help a bit by charging you under Article 99, *misbehavior before the enemy.* Then all you'd have to do is prove you behaved in a manner fitting your position. I.e., you shot him."

"Like I said, Major, I don't know what sort of defense Major Sullivan is planning."

"Well, there's Article 109, *destruction of other than military property.* That's pretty straightforward. Of course, the General can claim that, being his, Ludwig was military property, in which case we go with Article 108."

"Sounds like you have lots of choices," Peterson said.

"There's more, son. There's Article 104, *dueling.* Article 116, *riot or breach of peace.* Article 117, *provoking speeches or gestures.* And if that isn't enough, there's the last one, Article 134, *the general article.*"

"He gets his own?"

"What? No. It's worded in such a way to cover any omissions in the other fifty-seven. I just fill in the blanks. If we were doing this for real, I think that's the one a lawyer would use."

"Then why not use it?"

"I'm trying to find the one that carries the smallest sentence," Mayse said. "And one you can beat."

"I like dueling," Peterson said.

"I do, too. It's got a ring to it. A romantic gesture, and all that. But at the heart of dueling there's honor, and it might be better to avoid all that."

"Honor, huh?"

"Your judge ain't got none, unless I miss my guess."

"Arm-bruiser," Peterson said, and looked as if he'd weep.

"Arm-bruiser," Mayse agreed. "This is a bad thing."

The two of them sat in that small hot room for a couple of minutes without speaking. Mayse was thinking the Marine Corps had fallen a long ways and was on hard times. God alone knew what Peterson was thinking.

"You know Armbruster?" Mayse asked.

Peterson nodded. "I get mess duty a lot."

"Well, see, there's ground for appeal right there."

Peterson thought some more. "What would you do if you was me, sir?" he finally asked.

"I don't know, Peterson. I really don't. But if you like, I'll give it some thought."

Peterson stood up. "I'd like that. Thank you."

"I'll look you up in a day or two," Mayse said, "if I come to any answers."

Peterson, at the door, said, "Maybe the V.C. did it."

"Why would Charlie shoot Ludwig?"

"Lunch?" Peterson asked.

"Are you telling me you didn't do it?"

"That's what I've been telling you all along, sir."

"Why don't I believe you?"

"I guess because I look like someone that might shoot the General's dog."

"Yup," Mayse said, "I guess that's why."

Peterson went out, and the Major flipped back through his *Manual for Courts-Martial*. "Article 102," he said to himself, *"forcing a safeguard."*

Mayse decided that if he were Peterson he'd tell the General he did it and take his time in the brig. But he'd already suggested that, and he knew that young men didn't think that way. Peterson would probably rather be in the bush. So the trial began at 0900 Monday morning in blanket supply. The blankets had been removed and chairs inserted. Outside it was hot and raining, the worst weather for men and machinery. The hut, bare now except for three tables and six chairs, smelled of mildew and wet wool.

Mayse had a hundred dollars on Peterson at odds of 9/2 against. The General, Mayse heard, had a thousand going the other way, and it was pretty clear that a certain over-the-hill major would have to be very stupid to lose a general that much money. Mayse hoped Peterson hadn't bet on himself.

Peterson appeared in Class-A's that hung on him like a tent. His left shirt pocket was naked except for the fire watch ribbon and rifle expert badge. His sleeves were empty of rank. His eyes, Mayse thought, empty of hope.

The cook, Armbruster, still in his mess whites, walked to the front of the small room and pounded on the table with a hammer. "This here court's in session," he said.

"Mock court," Mayse said.

"What's that, Major?"

"Mock court," Mayse repeated. "This isn't a real trial. Didn't they tell you that?"

"Am I the judge, here, or ain't I?"

"I guess you are, Sergeant."

"Then this here court's in session." He put a dent in the table. "The accused will stand up and tell us his name."

"Peterson," Peterson said.

"The book says you got to give your whole name," Armbruster said.

"Alan Peterson."

"In a military fashion." Armbruster pointed his hammer.

"Peterson," Peterson said. "Alan B. Private, U.S. Marine Corps. Eight-three-nine-nine-oh-four-seven."

"Are you aware of the charges against you?"

"No."

"Don't screw around, Peterson."

"I'm not screwing around."

Everyone looked at Major Mayse.

Mayse stood up. He cleared his throat. "Uh. The accused, Private Peterson, is being charged under Article 109 of the Uniform Code of Military Justice, viz. and to wit: that he did, at 2nd Marines Staging Area, Hoc Lo, in the Republic of South Vietnam, on or about the 29th of April, 1967, without proper authority, willfully destroy by shooting with an M-16, Ludwig, a four-year-old Doberman pinscher then belonging to Brigadier General Harold Hilling, U.S. Marine Corps, of a value of about three hundred dollars, not military property of the United States." Mayse took a breath. "And that's about it."

"How do yóu plead, Peterson?"

Major Sullivan stood up, hungover. "Guilty," he said.

"Not guilty," said Peterson.

"Which is it?" asked the cook.

"Not guilty," said Sullivan. He'd forgotten he was the defense.

Armbruster took a piece of paper out of his pocket, unfolded it carefully, and turned it right side up. He seemed to be reading laboriously. Finally, he said, "Opening arguments?"

"I don't have one," Mayse said.

"Then I don't, either," said Sullivan.

"Presentation of evidence," Armbruster read.

"I don't have any of that, either," Mayse said. "The evidence is buried."

"You buried evidence?"

Mayse nodded.

"Isn't that illegal?"

"It seemed like the thing to do at the time."

"Oh," Armbruster looked at Major Sullivan, who shrugged. "Look, Peterson," the cook said, pointing his hammer, "did you shoot the dog, or dintcha?"

"I dintch."

"Well, *someone* shot the damn dog," Sullivan said, getting to his feet again.

"Yeah," said the cook. "Someone shot the damn dog."

"It wasn't me."

"Everybody knows it *was* you."

"I can't find anyone to corroborate that," Major Mayse said.

"What's that?"

"I can't find anyone to corroborate that," he said again.

"What's that, *corroborate*?"

"It means," Mayse said, "that while everyone might know it, no one can prove it." The cook looked blank. "No one saw him do it."

"So?"

"So there's no evidence."

"Well, of course there ain't no goddamn evidence. You already told me you buried it." Armbruster turned on Peterson. "Dintcha tell Maggot and Smokin' Earl you were going to off the CG's dog?"

"I don't remember."

"And then the next day, when the dog was offed, dintcha tell everyone that you done it?"

"I don't think so," Peterson said. "That would've been pretty stupid."

"Well, of course it was stupid. If you're going to off the General's friggin' dog, you do it quiet. With poison or somethin'. Gunpowder, maybe, in his chow, or—"

"I hate to interrupt, Sergeant," Mayse said. "This is interesting as hell and all. But trying the case is up to me, and *I don't have a case*."

"You've got to," Sullivan said. "I want to defend him."

"*I've* got a case."

Mayse swiveled with the rest of them to look. General

"Hammerhead" Hilling, a short, square, bald man, glittered in the doorway. He walked in and took the empty chair next to Mayse and said, "I'm ready to testify."

"You saw Peterson shoot your dog, sir?"

"I did."

The cook sat down, satisfied.

Mayse sighed and opened his briefcase. He pulled a Bible out and scooted it over to the General. "Sir, do you swear to tell the truth, the whole truth, and nothing but the truth regarding the matter before us?"

"Of course not."

"Of course not, sir?"

"Hell, no, mister. I'm a general. I don't need a Bible. And, anyway, this is a practice, a run-through. Didn't Major Sullivan make that clear?"

"Yes, sir, he did."

"Well, then, save the swearing for the real thing."

"Yes, sir."

"What time was the shot fired?"

"The guard says about 2315, sir."

"That's right. Twenty-three hundred, a little after. I was out, near the"—he shot a look at Sullivan—"PX?"—Sullivan nodded—"the PX, looking for Ludwig, when this maniac rushed out, took a bead on him, and blew him away. Dog didn't have a chance." The General shook his head, heartbroken. He got up, staring at the back of Peterson's head. "Call me when you're ready for sentence. And get *on* with it."

With the General gone, the court was over, but it took Armbruster a minute to figure that out. "Either of you majors got anything more to say?"

They shook their heads.

"Then I'm going to impose sentence."

"You've got to find him guilty, first," Mayse said.

The cook stared at him. "Weren't you listening?"

"You've still got to do it."

"All right, guilty. That please you? Guilty. Now give me five minutes to think up something good."

"The most he can get is thirty days and reduction in rank," Mayse said.

"You ain't the judge, I am."

Mayse surrendered.

"Court's recessed for five minutes, or until I call you." The hammer came down. Nobody moved. At last, Armbruster got up and went out into the rain.

"That's that," Sullivan said.

"Wasted half an hour," Mayse agreed.

"He can't give me thirty days, can he?" Peterson asked.

"Hell, yes," Sullivan said.

"No, Peterson, he can't. The General was asleep in his quarters; I checked. The most that will happen is that you'll get a trial. And that won't happen, either."

The five minutes turned into fifteen. Peterson got up and stared out the window. Sullivan went to sleep. The General came back in and sat down next to Mayse. "You hashed that up," he said. The cook came in wearing a cartridge belt and a sidearm. "With your permission, General?" he asked.

"Go on ahead, son," General Hilling said. "Hang him."

"No, sir. We're going to shoot him." The cook looked pleased with himself. "The accused will rise."

Peterson stood up, looking desperately at Mayse.

"Wait a minute," Mayse said.

"Shut up," said the General. "And sit down. I like this."

"Private Peterson," Armbruster said, "this court finds you guilty of shooting General Hilling's beloved dog, Ludwig. And since it happened in a theater of combat operations while that noble beast"—here he turned to the General with a little bow—"was in the performance of his military duties in the face of the enemy, this court ain't got no choice but to sentence you to death in front of the firing squad."

Armbruster pulled the .45 from its holster and looked at it. "In other words, dickhead—excuse me, General—what goes around, comes around." He pulled the slide back and chambered a round. He had his thumb on the hammer. "Any last words, Peterson?"

"This isn't right," Peterson said.

"Wait a minute, Armbruster," Mayse said.

"Yes—" the General began.

But the shot in that small room quieted everyone. Mayse looked at the smoke around the gun and turned to see Peterson slumped over against Sullivan. The General said, "Gah," and slumped over against Mayse. "Fork," he said, and passed out.

"Jesus Christ," Mayse said.

"Worked good, huh?" asked Armbruster. He holstered the weapon. "Ain't nothin' in it but blanks, Major. I made 'em myself."

"Get a medic, idiot," Sullivan said.

"I told you, sir, he's just fainted."

"Not for Peterson. I think you've killed the General."

Armbruster almost had killed the General. The medics took him off to the hospital and fed him oxygen. The MPs took statements from everyone and then arrested the cook. Sullivan wandered off to get some sleep. Mayse and Peterson sat in the empty room and looked at each other.

"Is it over?" Peterson asked.

"I doubt it."

Orders came down the next day shipping everyone—Mayse, Sullivan, Armbruster, and Peterson—to Echo Company, 1st Battalion, 2nd Marines. The bush.

Mayse was already packed.

And the day after that they shipped Major Mayse back to the staging area, as he'd always known would happen if he saw combat one more time, as stiff and cold as the Doberman, a bullet hole between his eyes.

MUTINY

Sir Quentin Tennant, K.C.B., D.S.O. and Bar, was carried on a litter from the sloop *Pegasus* to the hospital with a ringing in his ears. The high-pitched whine inside his head had begun three days before, when his island pilot had jumped overboard with the ship's chronometer, and Sir Quentin (at seventy, as frail as a bowsprit) had leaped in after him, and would have caught the man but for his own cursing, and so ended up, instead, swallowing enough seawater to drown a calmer man. The pilot got away. It wasn't the theft so much (though Sir Quentin was no thief's friend) as it was the chronometer: that was England! GMT—Time itself, by God!—and whether from the seawater he'd swallowed or the simple enormity of the crime, the buzzing began inside his brain.

On the fourth morning, when the humming streaked his vision like varnish and the world turned sideways, he picked up the ship-to-shore and asked for help. There's been a mutiny, he told the harbormaster. A piracy. The ship's balance is gone. And though the harbormaster thought he said ballast (how could that be?), he sent two natives out in their clean white trousers and tattooed chests to take him off in a dinghy.

From his bed in the hospital Sir Quentin could see, if he stretched, a fingernail of hillside and beach, and a white cross in the water that might be *Pegasus*. Stretching hurt; he lay back, suddenly old. His bed was a tubular cot, a crib with high sides that slid down, and it was the indecency of a bed like that, he thought, as much as anything that made him feel infirm. A mosquito net had been gathered up behind his head and was secured to the wall by a hook and a piece of old twine. An old Spitfire's propeller turned slowly overhead. The only other bed in the ward was unmade, its blue-striped mattress doubled over to expose chain-link rust from the springs: tiny figures-of-eight. Under the din of the turbine that ran in his brain he could hear office sounds from the next room.

The doctor who came in to look him over was too tall and thin and too young. Womanly hands were attached to the ends of his long arms. He stared at the clipboard he carried, apparently afraid to meet his patient's eyes.

"Howdy," he said, not looking up.

"Oh, dear God," said Sir Quentin. "I'm in America."

The doctor looked up then, but his glance bounced off the old man's face and traveled around the room, settling like a fly on the clipboard. "You're on Ovalau. In the Fijis. I'm Dr. Wilson, an American." He paused, as if considering how much more to say, and then said simply, "You have a medical emergency."

Sir Quentin sat up and settled himself more comfortably against the pillows and the crib's metal back. "Bells in the old brainbox, I'm afraid."

"Bells?"

"Ringing."

"Ringing in the ears, eh?"

"Right." Sir Quentin rolled the r.

"What does it sound like?" The boy doctor, practicing a professionalism that seemed newly adopted, struck an attitude that Sir Quentin took to be bored and unsympathetic.

Sir Quentin pulled on an earlobe and cocked his head, listening. "Zumzumzum," he said.

"Zum zum zum?"

"Faster."

"Zumzumzum?"

"Higher."

"Zum!zum!zum!"

"That's it exactly," Sir Quentin said, and smiled.

"Odd," the young doctor said, and made a note.

"Is it?"

"It?" He shook his head. "You," he said, turning, and walked out.

A nurse came in directly and strapped a pressure cuff on Sir Quentin's left arm and pumped it up. The constriction felt somehow pleasurable, and he was—unaccountably—angered by that.

"I've been asked by the doctor to take your medical history," she said, when she'd finished with his blood pressure.

"Quite all right," Sir Quentin said stiffly.

She was a lovely girl. It was Sir Quentin's experience that native girls were always lovely, no matter how homely others might find them. He was, he supposed, a xenophile. The Burmese girls he had known—young or old—had bright, friendly smiles, and even the large-footed, flat-faced girls of Tonga possessed a massive frailty that fascinated him. This Fijian lass, though (even with her short, American vowels), would be beautiful anywhere.

"Are you taking any medicines presently?" she asked.

"Digitalis," said Sir Quentin. "For the clockworks."

"Digitalis is for the heart." She pronounced each word carefully. The *g* in digitalis was French on her tongue.

He nodded and rapped his knuckles against his chest. "Clockworks," he agreed.

She smiled. "Your age, please?"

"Seventy."

"Seventy?"

"The twenty-fourth of July, last," he said. "I was born in 1914." He straightened so that his toes pointed at the end of the bed. "The year of the Great War."

"1914," she repeated, in a way that touched him.

"1914," he said again, awed himself. "Nearly a century ago."

"No, no," she said. "Not so long ago as that. My great-grandfather is ninety-one, and he still dances with me."

"The luck of some men exceeds all understanding," he said. And then, to her shy smile: "The elderly are held in high esteem, here, are they not? They are honored?"

She bowed her head. Not an Oriental gesture, he realized, but simply a feminine one.

"Address?" she whispered.

"Kensington Park. London. England."

"Great Britain?"

"Yes."

"You are a long way from home."

"Yes."

She wrote it down. "The address of your nearest living relative, please?"

"Do you think that I'm likely to die here?"

"I beg your pardon?" She looked down at her feet. The part in her dark hair was fine and straight.

"Pardon me," he said. "That was inexcusable."

"It's a question on the form, sir. I must ask it."

"I know. Please forgive me."

She looked up and allowed her smile to return.

"My son, Edward," he said. "He lives in New York, in America." He gave her the address.

"New York, and London," she said.

"Yes. New York and London." He understood.

"One last address, please. Here in the Islands?"

"*Pegasus*. A white sloop in the harbor."

"Oh, I think I've seen it. It's quite beautiful."

"Thank you."

She asked him about a number of ailments, to which he replied that he'd had the misfortune to acquire malaria and hepatitis.

"That's fine," she said.

"I beg your pardon?"

"The mosquitoes here carry Dengue Fever. You will be immune."

"I am immune to nearly everything," he said. "I have walked barefooted on hot coals. I have been bitten by the cobra."

"You are lucky to have survived the cobra," she said. "That is a terrible snake."

"Have you seen one?"

She shook her head.

He buried his chin against his chest in an effort to flatten the soft skin at his neck. She laughed at his attempt.

"A terrible snake," he agreed. "They can spit, like camels."

She nodded. "And they blind."

"Yes." One had blinded him.

"And they are most venomous."

"Yes." The agony of it rushed back, unwelcome, unbidden. He forced a smile. "But I am immune."

"Pardon me?"

"Yes. The native doctor who saw to my wounds assured me I had immunity from the cobra."

"That is incorrect."

"Are you certain?"

"Quite certain. If you had been bitten a second time, you would have died without an antivenin. That you survived the first bite is something of a miracle."

She was looking at him so gravely that he believed her immediately, but still he asked again, "Are you certain?"

She nodded. "It is the truth."

Sir Quentin leaned back against the wall and closed his eyes. She leaned forward and delicately laid a hand on his cheek.

"Surely there's nothing to worry about," she said. "You couldn't have been bitten here. We have no snakes in Fiji."

Sir Quentin said nothing.

"Are you all right, sir?"

"What? *All right?*" Sir Quentin couldn't bring her into focus. He barely heard her through the thrumming. "Yes," he said, finally. "I'm fine. I'm fine."

"You don't look well."

The noise inside quieted a bit, and the longer he thought about what she'd said, the funnier it became. He allowed himself a chuckle, and then a laugh, and the nurse joined him. They both sat back, smiling.

"What's your name, dear?"

"Joy," she said shyly.

"There is a remarkable felicity in names," Sir Quentin said.

"Thank you, Mr. Tennant." She was pleased; she couldn't hide it.

"Quentin."

"Oh, no. I couldn't. Please. Mr. Tennant."

"As you wish."

She finished the history and then remained in the chair by the bed, apparently comfortable in doing nothing, or perhaps with nothing else to do. Sir Quentin hiked up the pillows. Their eyes kept missing each other; she looked at his ears, he looked at her throat. It was delicate, finely chiseled, decorated with a tiny gold cross.

She took a deep breath (it gave Sir Quentin a start: her youthful loveliness gave him quick, sinless pleasure and a quick, momentary guilt) and then she said, leaning forward, "What is London like? And New York? Have you been to America?"

London, he thought, is the only real city on Earth. America is full of cowards and dishonorable men. But he said, instead, "America is a beautiful puzzle. Like Eden, it is a garden populated by malcontents and criminals." He saw the shock on her face and hurried on, cursing himself. "But it is somehow still wonderful," he said.

He told her of America (the little he'd seen of it) and then, more slowly, of an England he had mostly never seen, one that had been drawn for him by his father two-thirds of a century earlier: a bedtime-story England, shut up in glory and darkness, where knights performed valorous deeds and dragons lurked, still, up in the mountains of Wales—an England he longed for, always, and always would.

He had traveled much of the world when he was a young man and he was now busy traveling the rest of it, and he teased her with exotic names, knowing he did, but not knowing that Pago Pago and Kuala Lumpur and Bangkok didn't interest her in the least: it was San Francisco she longed for, and Los Angeles.

It tired him finally. She stopped him gently just before he

would have stopped himself. "Thank you," she said, rising. She laid a cool hand on his arm. "I must go, and you must rest."

He nodded and closed his eyes in the delicious, languid warmth of a Fiji afternoon and slipped into sleep with the humming of bees outside his window. Or perhaps, he thought drowsily, the bees were in his head.

Sir Quentin and Joy spent two days in quiet conversation while blood tests were run and his ears were examined by an older, Indian doctor, who was called over from Viti Levu at Sir Quentin's insistence. "I see nothing wrong," the older doctor said, "but we will wait for the tests."

So Sir Quentin told Joy of Rome, and of Egypt during the war, and how he remembered the Greek islands baking in white heat on water that looked painted. In the midst of these reminiscences the boy doctor, against his nature (and for no reason Sir Quentin could fathom), challenged him to a back-gammon game, but then grew impatient with the old gentleman's deliberations over the dice and invented an excuse to leave. The backgammon board, now, still with its pieces in battle, waited on a small table under the window.

And Sir Quentin talked about America, to Joy's gentle prodding. He had to guess at things, to make up stories, and he began most of them with something to the effect of: "The Colonials overthrew their rightful government, that is, the King." Joy would nod and wait for him to move up through the centuries. "A disrespectful lot," he said. She nodded some more.

When he refused anymore to talk about America—lies, even harmless ones, bothered him—she asked, as he knew she must, about his son.

"A snake in the grass," Sir Quentin said softly. He raised two empty hands and looked up into the shadows of the ancient banyan tree they sat under. "My son is a burden to me."

"He's a bad man?" Joy asked. She first looked stricken and

then disbelieving as her lips began to curl into a smile. "*Your son?*"

Sir Quentin slumped a little in the chair, knowing he was being melodramatic, but figuring, rightly, that that is a prerogative of age. "Edward was born in New York City," he said in a tone that made it clear that that was his son's first mistake (which is what he did think, though how he could assign that responsibility to a newborn infant baffled even him). "You see, his mother was—is—American, and she wanted her child to have a choice of citizenship. She went back to her home when she was with child."

"Is it not she, then, who is a"—she paused—"a snake-in-the-grass?" It sounded wonderful the way she said it. Ah, Eden.

He shook his head. "My son is a coward," he said sadly, and was shocked to find that he could admit this to anyone else. Perhaps it was her innocence that drew it out. He rushed on, now that he had begun. "I can accept cowardice in the rest of the world—in fact, I've come to expect it—but not in my own son. In my own son . . ." He shook his head again, something that had become a tic in the last few days.

"What did he do?"

"It's more a case of all he didn't do," Sir Quentin said.

The crucible of courage was war, Sir Quentin believed, and to be fair, there hadn't been one for his son when it was needed. But Edward didn't fight back when he was bullied—even as a child, this was clear—and wouldn't defend his friends when defense was wanted, and, worst of all, chose not to stand up to his father's displeasures, but meekly accepted his terrible monthly rages. Awful. It made them worse, of course. He had gone back as a young man with his father's blessings to live with his mother for a while in New York, but he never returned, and he gave up forever his right to live under the Crown. She had never come back, either. He stopped just short of telling Joy that.

"He left you, then," Joy said. "He has betrayed you."

"Yes," he said, surprised.

"Like America."

He didn't hear that last part; he was thinking of betrayal. He had believed—until he lost his son—that courage was a matter of breeding: that it was inherited.

He had looked back through the genealogy of his wife's family for clues to the trouble, but had found none. Her father had been decorated in the Great War, and her grand-father, as a boy, had distinguished himself in the War between the States. His son, he was forced to decide, must be some sort of sad mutant whose good breeding on both sides had gone horribly wrong and who had disgraced them all. Through those years of looking for a reason, he heard his own father's warning in his ears: Don't marry a Yank. But he had, and was sorry for it.

He looked up to see Joy watching him, still waiting for an answer.

"I don't know anything more about America," he said. "Let me tell you something of India." That colony, too, well . . . never mind.

When he had been in the hospital a week and the doctors could find nothing physically wrong, Sir Quentin was dis-charged. The ringing in his ears had lessened somewhat, al-though he still had to concentrate when someone spoke, had to strain the words through the zumzumzum that was still with him. The boy doctor wasn't able to tell him whether it was a permanent condition, but suggested he see a specialist in one of the larger cities: Sydney, in Australia, or Auckland, in New Zealand, if he was sailing that far. Sir Quentin took an affectionate farewell from Joy, paid the reckoning, and went back aboard the *Pegasus*.

He found he had no balance left, and *Pegasus* was no longer large enough for him. He'd lost his sea legs for good. The small, gentle motion of the sloop at anchor in the quiet bay sent him reeling, clutching at lines and bulkhead stanchions, and twice he nearly fell overboard. "The insidiousness of this disease," he called out loudly to no one, "will take everything from me." He rigged storm lines across the deck and tried to make do.

The exaggerated motion he felt not only frightened him, but sickened him as well. He crouched in the small cabin all day with his hands clenched around a brass counter rail, and when it grew dark enough so that he couldn't be seen, he sneaked ashore and slept on the beach. He didn't go back to the boat in the morning, but climbed instead up into the hills until he found a clear view of the harbor and his sloop. He stared at it resting peacefully in the mirror of the harbor and wondered what he had come to.

He lay back and let the jungle bamboozle him. He stared into the dark branches of a tree and thought of Eden, of Camelot, where men were created pure (not by accident!) and then savaged by the snake. Why? Jealousy. Bitterness. Envy. Cowardice. Greed. He wanted to live.

He was seized by a memory of such astonishing clarity that the buzzing in his ears stopped and he was back in a village in Burma, at the beginning of the Second World War.

The fighting hadn't quite got there, yet. Rumors ricocheted among the men and heavy guns rumbled in the mountains, but his orders were to stand fast, to wait and see. Sir Quentin hadn't yet been knighted by the King for his action at Sadiya Pass—he had not yet heard of the place, nor could he imagine that terrible bottleneck filled with Japanese soldiers bayonet-to-bayonet with his own small detachment of rear guard troops—he hadn't yet been promoted and given a command of his own, or in any way distinguished himself from among the other young officers of good family.

But then he was blinded by the cobra, and all that changed. He was shaving at the edge of the jungle when the snake reared up out of the bamboo and spat in his eyes. He backed away, screaming, digging at the acid with his fingers. He stumbled and fell. The snake lashed into his bare arm and then was gone into the tall grass.

A rock under his spine forced his back into a bow, and he remembered the scent of shaving soap and the smear of lather still in the palm of one hand. The morning sun caught the mirror he'd hung, and he kept its light in his eye because it drove the pain out, and then a boy knelt beside him and cut him just below the shoulder with his own razor, and set his mouth to the wound and drew out the blood, and two others stood over him and unwound their loincloths. He felt their warm streams on his face and tried to turn away but couldn't—that rock—and smelled, then tasted, the pungent urine that ran down both cheeks, cutting channels through the shaving soap, while the one boy stayed at his shoulder, sucking at his biceps like a pump, and someone— one of his own men—blocked the mirror, put him in the shade, and allowed the pain its hold.

A native doctor told him later that the cobra's venom blinds unless washed away by uric acid and that those three boys had saved his sight and his life. He had leaned up on his good arm from the cot in his tent and looked at the three brown faces as the boys crowded around him, their smiles caught like light in the mirror, and he gave them each a shiny new sixpence. They bowed and backed out. The doctor nodded approvingly and told Sir Quentin he need never again fear the cobra.

So in his boyishness, his bravado, he'd searched cobras out in villages and marketplaces and made a point of handling the shiny, mottled beasts, to the delight of his fellow officers, and the men under him, and to his own glory. He quickly gained a reputation for courage, which he began to believe in himself, and the rest of war unwound as it had to: promotions, medals, the Honors List; but now, forty-five years after the event, first in the hospital with Joy and now on the hillside overlooking the harbor, he realized that his courage was the product of that native doctor's lie, or ignorance, and that he was a brave man by mistake.

"Oh, Edward!" Sir Quentin cried. "Oh, Edward. Edward, my son!"

A rain began, and Sir Quentin crawled on his hands and knees for shelter, then pulled himself up under an old banyan with its roots draped from its branches, held on to them like a prisoner, and wept.

They brought him back to the same bed, in that same hospital, and he looked up at that slowly spinning airplane propeller and heard clearly in the other room the typewriter noises and the telephone ringing. When Joy came in, he took her hand and held on tightly. The war, in some mysterious loop of time, was with him again.

He had no balance at all and felt, lying in bed, as if he were standing. The room would rock, gently, as if he were at sea again in *Pegasus,* and the light that came through the open window was a Burmese light, soft as flowers, and the fighting in the hills, though growing closer, was still very far away.

He had trouble seeing. Objects lost their sharpness. Joy's tiny gold cross was a blur of light, and her lovely dark eyes were spots that swam in front of his. The zumzumzum never returned, but all other sounds faded and the room grew dark, with afternoon, he thought, and although he no longer felt Joy's hand in his he was sure it was there.

Sir Quentin Tennant cried out for his son, wishing to be allowed one more hour with him, to ask for his forgiveness, and then he cried out to Joy and called her Elizabeth, and then he called out for the doctor, for help, but knew he wasn't heard. In that moment the dignity of death he'd taken for granted for nearly half a century was revealed to him as a sham: regardless of what others saw, a man's gentility, bred in the blood or conferred with a sword, deserted him at this time. He shrugged off the fraud he had wrapped around his life and found, in the face of a consuming power more final than any cobra's, that he was indeed fit.

STUPID-PROOF

Charlie coasted up to me in that quiet way of his and sat down on the grass and opened his lunch bucket. He finished one bologna sandwich and was making good inroads on another before he told me he'd been fired from the bottle company that morning.

"Why's that?"

"I dunno." He shrugged and stuffed the rest of the sandwich in sideways. "Firf thang thif—"

"Wait," I said, and held up a hand.

He chewed, obediently, and then reached over and took the rest of my Coke to wash it down. "First thing this morning," he said, "Mr. Chambers called me into his office at nine straight up and said I could take my pay and go. 'Livia had the check made out."

"Did he tell you why?"

Charlie shook his head.

"Did you ask?"

He shook it again.

"Why not?"

"If they don't want me," he said, "then I don't want to stay. The reason don't make no difference."

"Did you break any bottles?"

"Yup." He drove a hand into his lunch bucket and came out with a banana.

"Lots of them?"

"I guess so."

"Pitchin' baseballs at 'em?"

"Naw. I don't do that anymore." He peeled the banana down to its nothing and offered me half, to pay for the Coke. "I think prob'ly it has to do with 'Livia—the new girl that works in the office?"

I nodded, helping him on.

"She's been eating lunch with Mr. Chambers."

"So?"

"In his office. Way past lunch time. I saw 'em the other day when I was cleaning the windows."

"They have you cleaning windows?"

"Sometimes."

"And they weren't eating lunch?"

"Not really."

"And they saw you?"

"I guess they did. I knocked on the glass and waved."

"Oh, Charlie."

"She's got legs that don't quit. And boobs—" He held his hand out so I could appreciate the boobs she had.

"Yeah, well, that ought to have done it," I said. "Didn't you think that might get you fired?"

He shook his head. "I wouldn't mind someone watchin' if it was me that had 'Livia upside down on my desk."

I tried to keep the picture out of my head, but it came anyway: long-legged, dark-haired Olivia and fat, bald, old Mr. Chambers.

"Pointy," Charlie said.

"What?"

"Her boobs. And her bra loaded in the front. I didn't know they had those."

"They have those," I said, and sat up, and drew my skirt over my knees. "Did you ever think, Charlie, that no matter what Mr. Chambers thought about it—and you're wrong, by the way; he wouldn't be pleased—*Olivia* might mind being spied on?"

"Nope."

"Well, she probably did. And *Mrs.* Chambers would mind a lot."

"Yeah, I thought of that."

"Well, good for you." Mrs. Chambers had the money and the kind of temper that people with money can usually control, and it's a cinch she would have straight-out killed her husband with a meat-ax or a hammer and taken her chances in court. I told Charlie that.

"Then he fired me in self-defense," he said slowly. He nodded when he had it for sure. "He was saving his own life."

"It's probably not saved, yet, until you're out of the county altogether."

"I ain't leavin'."

"I don't want that, either, Charlie. Don't spread that story around."

"Okay," he said. "I won't tell it anymore."

"Any more?"

He grinned at me. "There's been a weekend between then and now."

I let myself fall back on the grass. I spread my fingers to shade my eyes. "Oh, Charlie. You need a job—no, a place, *a whole town*—that's stupid-proof."

"What does that mean?"

"It means someplace where you can't get in trouble."

"The only place like that is baseball," he said. "And I didn't do too good there, either."

"You did fine at the baseball part," I said, and patted his knee. "Nobody threw 'em any harder."

Charlie had pitched high school ball in Binghamton, up in New York, where the Yankees had a triple A club, and they'd signed him and sent him down here to Owensboro in the Kitty League. They'd had big plans for him. He had a great fastball, a good slider and off-speed pitch, and a lightning move to first. His hitting was fair. He worked hard. He got along with everybody. Except Ralph Dugan.

I'd gone to school with Ralph, and I can testify with my hand on my grandmother's Bible that he was a jerk. Ralph was short and wide and the kind of man you can't put into any kind of uniform. We have our share of those around here, or used to—mostly deputies—but Ralph was the worst. If they'd ever strapped a gun on him he would have shot old men for crossing against the light, and I guess we're lucky he was just an umpire in the A league. He and Charlie had disliked each other right from the go.

I told Charlie to ignore him, that he'd be pitching double A ball and then triple A back home up in Binghamton, and then he'd be in the majors in Yankee Stadium, in the rotation with Whitey Ford, and that Ralph wouldn't go any farther than Owensboro calling balls and strikes on kids just out of high school. You can put up with him for a spring and summer, I told him—maybe not even that long—but Charlie said he couldn't put up with him another day and the next game that Ralph Dugan was behind the plate Charlie beaned him twice and put him out. The catcher, Scotty Reynolds, had a lot to do with that, but they never even fined him. I saw Dugan's mask, and Charlie had *broken* it.

Ralph, the next game in his normal turn, went on to umpire at first, and Charlie got him there, too, keeping a runner close, and that time he was in the hospital a week. They would have sent Charlie down, if there had been a down to send him to, but they talked to him instead and made him promise to leave Dugan alone.

Dugan should have left Charlie alone. When he got back into the game a week later he leaned on Charlie more than ever. One late afternoon Dugan was watching the bag at third when someone tried to steal it. Charlie had to balk to get him. Most people agree, however, that it was the finest damn throw they'd ever seen. He whirled and threw it underhanded, blind, and the third baseman, Billy Briggs, picked the ball up off the rebound—one hollow bounce off Dugan's skull—and tagged the runner out. Charlie was a favorite in this town for thirty seconds until the other umpires ran up and got it straightened out, called the balk and made the runner safe, and carried Ralph Dugan into the dugout. After they did that, Ralph sagging in the middle between the two of them like a butchered hog, Charlie was a born-in-the-bone Southern

Hero. If we gave out medals in this town, we would have given them all to him.

The Yankees let him go. Ralph Dugan was in the hospital, that time, three weeks. He is now a shy, quiet man who has lost about eighty pounds and works for the Civic Betterment Committee, planting shrubs and such. Most of us agree Charlie did him a favor.

"Do you remember Ralph Dugan?" I asked Charlie.

"Sure. I see him around once in a while."

"You get along with him?"

"Sure. Why not?"

"He took you out of baseball."

"Naw," Charlie said, and joined me, flat on the grass. He shielded his eyes, too. "*I* took me out of baseball."

I gave his knee another pat. "There's hope for you, buddy."

"You don't need to worry, Kip," he said. "I learned that lesson—what is it?—twenty-five years ago."

"About that."

"You drummed it into my head."

"Good."

"You came to every game, didn't you?"

"I saw you throw your first pitch."

"Really?" He sat up.

"Fastball to Clive 'Warthog' McKittrick. He popped it up."

"*I* don't even remember my first pitch."

"You don't take an interest in your career like I do," I said.

"Kip." He rolled over, half on top of me. I pushed him off.

"We've been through that," I said. "And past it. It didn't make you happy, remember?"

"Yeah, but I can't remember why."

"'Cause I kept pushing you," I said, "to do something with your life."

"Yeah, that's right; you did."

That sort of dumb ambition got in the way of love, and lovemaking. I had been a whole lot unhappier than Charlie but it had rubbed off on him until he thought he was the one who was miserable, and I gave him half a dozen reasons to leave, and then when I finally had to show him one, he got the message. I know exactly what my faults are and where they lie. I'd wanted Charlie to make something of himself the first day I saw him tossing warm-up pitches in the bullpen, ever since I saw him tug that cap over his eyes and maul that baseball in his big hands. I learned baseball because of him; if he'd been a lawyer and I'd been in court, I would have learned law. I would have married him and had his children, if that's what he wanted, but all he'd wanted to do was pitch, and unfortunately, he'd wanted to pitch at umpires.

"You could have been great, kid."

"Naw."

There isn't any pain in those old memories for him, but they still hurt me like knives. I crabbed around onto one elbow and looked at my watch.

"I should be getting back," I said.

"Okay."

"What are you going to do now?"

"Walk over to the river, I guess," he said.

"I meant with your life, Charlie. What are you going to do for a job?"

"I dunno."

"Is there any place in town you haven't worked?"

"I guess not," he said. "The bottling plant was about the last place left."

"What are you, Charlie, forty-eight?"

"You know I am. You know my birthday. You know more about me than I do."

I got up and twisted my skirt to fit and brushed the grass from its seat. "I'll think of something," I said. "Be home tonight. I'll call you."

I would have found him a job with me, at the bank, except we handle other people's money.

I tried for the rest of the day and most of that evening to find a way around the injustice of a man being built for just one purpose—throwing baseballs—and not being able to find a place to do it. So few of us have even one talent, it was criminal to see it wasted all these years.

While I was cooking—and trying to cook up something—my cat brought in a mouse, one of the new, spring mice that don't know anything about cats. He let it go in the kitchen. He gives them a sporting chance: they have my house to hide in. It doesn't bother me, so long as he takes them back outside for the butchering. I ate, watching with half an eye as that old black tomcat stalked his own dinner and then carried it out onto the back steps with his bent tail high, proud, the gray lump struggling feebly. Cat and mouse. Pitcher and umpire. It suddenly occurred to me that Ralph Dugan wasn't the only one who had ended up docile and beaned.

I called Charlie.

"I've had a thought," I said.

"What is it?"

"I don't want to tell you over the phone."

I waited, counting the seconds on my fingers. "Should I come over?" he finally asked, on the count of eight.

"If you want to hear what it is."

I heard his unmuffled pickup two blocks away and walked out onto the porch to wait for it. His headlights cut through the dark—one high, one low and sideways—then they lit up the yard as he pulled into the driveway and let the truck idle. It shook the windows behind me.

I drew a finger across my throat and he leaned out, waved, and shut the engine off. It shuddered and coughed for a minute before it died.

"Choke's stuck," he said. "I like to kick it a couple of times till it runs smooth before I shut it off."

"I don't have enough windows for that."

"What's your idea?"

"Come inside and have a beer."

He thunked down into the big easy chair in front of the television and put his feet up on my coffee table. "This is a nice place," he said.

"Do you know you've been coming over here for twenty-odd years, putting your feet up on my coffee table, and saying this is a nice place?"

"I guess I have."

I nodded along with him. "Even when you lived here. Next you'll be asking what kind of beer I've got."

"Bud?"

I had to smile. The past didn't stick with him like it does with others. Maybe that's not always all that bad.

"I want you to try and remember someone," I said, when he had his beer and I had mine and we were both comfortable. "It's a lot of years ago, back when you were pitching for Owensboro."

"Who is it?"

"The guy who took Ralph Dugan out of umpiring."

"That was me."

"No, it was an eighteen-year-old kid named Charlie Beck who had a great fastball and could have been a starter for the Yankees. Dugan called his strikes balls and balked a runner over whenever he could get away with it. This kid Charlie Beck didn't have a lot of brains, but he knew enough to know when he was getting screwed, and he did something about it."

"Yeah, that was me."

"Whatever happened to him? I keep looking in the sports pages, but it seems he's disappeared."

"What are you talking about, Kip? This is *me*."

I leaned back into the sofa with my beer and stared at him. I don't care how much rock there is in a man's skull, a woman's look will bore through it like a slow laser with enough time.

"You mean I don't throw fastballs anymore," he said slowly.

"I mean you don't play hardball anymore. Someone fires you, you quit."

He smiled. "That's funny."

"It's not funny, Charlie. The Cubs wanted you after the Yankees turned you loose, but you didn't even show up for their camp."

"That was because of you."

He said it so softly that I wasn't sure what it was he'd said for a minute. I put the beer down and got up and leaned over the back of his chair and hugged him. "Okay," I said just as quietly, "but the Yankees have just turned you loose again and this time I'm not in the way."

"What do you want me to do?"

"I want you to ask for your job back."

"Mr. Chambers won't give it to me."

"Don't be too sure." I got cross-legged on the sofa. "All he can do is fire you, and he's already done that. His wife can kill him."

You could watch it sink in, like a rock in Jello. It would be funny if I didn't love him so.

"You want me to blackmail him?"

"Well, yeah, sort of. But it's not really blackmail, Charlie. You don't have to threaten anything. Just walk in and ask for your job back."

"And he'll give it to me?"

"I think so, yes."

"Because of what I *could* do?"

"Something like that. Maybe because you asked for it. Maybe just out of fairness."

He finished his beer and leaned forward, with his elbows on his knees, trying to understand. "How's that?"

"Knocking on the window and waving showed a lack of judgment on your part, right?"

"I guess."

"What about what he was doing?"

"Yeah, so?"

"So you got fired. No one's firing him. Yet."

"Except Mrs. Chambers?"

"She doesn't even come into it. This is a matter of justice, pure and simple. If he wants to think of it the other way, let him."

"You think it'll work?"

"Yes, I do. I know it."

He stood up and dug his hands into his pockets and looked

down at his shoes. "Mr. Chambers," he said, "I want to be rehired."

"Ball, Charlie."

He straightened, firmed up his voice, and pulled one hand and then the other out. God, they were huge. "Miss 'Livia," he said tipping an invisible hat, "Mr. Chambers. I've come to get my job *back*."

"Down the middle."

He grinned and looked as if he were going to kiss me, but he hugged me instead and walked out to his truck. He stood at the open driver's-side door and shouted, "Miss 'Livia! Mr. Chambers! I've come for my job!"

"Strike, Charlie. On the corner!" I hollered.

He waved, started his truck, and drove out.

He got his job back, "without any argument," he said, and I lost mine two weeks later.

I guess it's no secret in this town that I am Charlie Beck's number-one fan. And it's no secret, either, that Charlie doesn't make decisions very often on his own. Owensboro Bottling has a lot of money in our bank, and Chambers plays poker with the man I used to work for. My boss, Argus, owed me a little less, I guess, than he owed Chambers. I'd forgotten, talking to Charlie that night, how small towns work, but I don't mind saying I wouldn't have done things any differently, anyway. As I had with Charlie years ago, you make your mistakes, and go on.

You swing through them. Stupid-proof is holding your head up and not letting your own stupidity beat you, but instead making it somehow, some way, accomplish something. After Charlie had beaned Dugan once, he beaned him again and again until he was gone from baseball, even though it had cost him a career. Charlie had known that once and had forgotten it. I had to learn it for myself, and then I still needed to have Charlie show me.

I called him after I'd worked through most of my self-pity, and in the course of the conversation I told him I'd been fired.

"Because of me," he said.

"No."

There was a long silence on his end, and then he said, "Come on by the plant at the end of the week, and I'll take you to lunch."

"I don't want to go to lunch," I said.

"Come on by, anyway."

I saw him Friday in the parking lot. He was driving a forklift of bottles. I waved, and he stopped and climbed down.

"Look here," he said, and took a bottle from an open crate. He held it up in the light. It was short, square—a whiskey bottle. "Looks a bit like Dugan, don't it?" he asked. "Or Chambers, either one."

He took it, and me, across the parking lot and into the scrub that bordered it. A post was driven into the ground about waist-high in a field of broken glass.

"You take girls to the nicest places," I said.

"Old jobs," he said, kicking into the pile and scattering the glass shards. "Past mistakes." He balanced the bottle on the post. "I've been throwing every day at lunch since I got back, and Chambers doesn't say anything about it. He hasn't even docked me for the breakage. Come over here."

He'd regained that confidence I'd fallen in love with nearly thirty years before. I walked with him away through the thistles and boxwood and fire ant nests and up onto a rise. "Sixty feet, six inches," he said. "Give me a pitch."

I held up one finger.

He reached down into the weeds and came up with a baseball, winked at me, wound up, and knocked the bottle off the post the first time.

"You always had a great arm," I said.

"That's not the point."

"There's a point?" I wasn't used to that from Charlie.

"There is," he said seriously. "You gave it back to me. The fire. The wanting to throw."

"Yes. Good. So?"

"So, what is it that you do?"

"I told you, Charlie; I've been fired."

"Everyone gets fired. What *did* you do?"

"I made loans."

"Right," he said. "Let's figure out who owes you."

He smiled at me. He stood on that homemade pitcher's mound and grinned like he was eighteen again, and after a minute I caught his drift and grinned back.

"I had another talk with Mr. Chambers," he said. "Seems 'Livia's going to find another job—in another county. Don't know why."

We grinned like conspirators.

"And Mr. Chambers expects you at work Monday morning."

"At my desk, or on it?" I asked.

"What?"

"Never mind. What's the job?"

He shrugged. "'Livia's. Something with figures."

Charlie would never understand his own humor. "Figures, huh?"

He nodded.

I looked at the glass mounds, glittering like ice in the heat, and I said, "I'll probably be the one who docks your pay for breakage."

THE SHORTEST HOLE

From the blue tees, it plays to fifty-nine yards. From the members' blocks, it plays to thirty-one. The ladies can reach it with a firm putt.

Nothing lies before the eye but green. It's no more than a chip, or in the foulest weather with the wind against, a pitch. No rocks threaten; no pond lurks.

Who'd build such a thing? you ask, such a bad joke of a hole, such an insult to the game?

Abernathy Hallistone is who. Abernathy Hallistone, the shrewdest architect living, a man with a heart like a triple bogey. Abernathy Hallistone, who understands as no one else the peculiar and torturous essence of the game of golf. Abernathy Hallistone, the *Scot.*

"You see," Hallistone will tell you, "the game's not in the hands. It's in the mind."

"But fifty-nine yards?"

"Consider, lad. Par won't feel good. Birdie is expected. And an ace? What do you put on the plaque in your office? *Hole-in-one. Half a sand wedge from half-a-hundred yards?* Where's the pride a man can take in that?" Here, he'll smile like the first freeze. "The ease of the hole inspires pure terror. I've watched entire foursomes take two to get on, and then, like as not, three putt. Double! And its placement on the course—the second hole—can ruin a *round.*"

But it can ruin more than a round. Abernathy Hallistone—architect from hell—decided to make the game easy and watch souls shatter.

One of these shattered souls took the name and shape of Ralph Fielding. Fielding, before playing the 2nd at Cragmore, had been happily successful and had believed in God.

Fielding played a sand wedge and knocked it over the green. He knocked it over again, coming back. He used a seven iron as a putter out of the rough and put it close, wondering all the while why he hadn't done so from the tee. Then, because of a deep, welling anger he didn't yet recognize as such, he missed his four-foot putt. Five. Five, on the easiest hole in the world, with sixteen more to go. He raised his putter above his head, bent it into an *omega* shape, and hurled it back at the tee. He'd have to choke up on his driver and putt with that.

Fielding choked up. The lowest score on his card when he was done was a six, and that on the truly easy, par-three 12th, normally a perfect eight iron from the tee without trouble. Fielding shot 121, and back at the clubhouse he broke his clubs and stuffed them into the barrel outside of the bar and then went inside to drink.

"How'd you hit 'em?" the bartender asked. He was twenty-one, new to the club, and oblivious to the luck that allowed him to live to see twenty-two.

Fielding said nothing.

"Have a good round?"

That sort of persistence can only lead to disaster. A low rumble began in the bottom of Fielding's feet.

"Nice weather for it," the bartender said. The club manager had told him to be friendly, but hell, this was work.

Soft gasping noises came from Fielding.

"Did you—"

"'*Nough!*" Fielding shouted, and that word—formed as it is high in the back of the palate—hurled with such force popped something vital behind Fielding's eyes, and he fell forward onto the bar's imitation mahogany like a landed fish.

"Jesus," the kid said, watching Fielding's hands twitch.

When Fielding got out of the hospital, he bought another set of clubs. He walked directly to the 2nd tee, elbowed his way silently through a waiting foursome, and, not appearing to notice their angry shouts (and perhaps he didn't), struck his ball with a seven iron.

He'd duffed it. He stared at the ball lying just off the tee, and then he turned, still without speaking, and dragged himself and his new clubs back to the 'house, where he broke each of them in turn and stuffed it into the barrel.

"Give me a double whiskey," he told the kid behind the bar, "and if you say a word to me, I'll kill you."

Thus began Ralph Fielding's decline.

Business dropped off. He couldn't make the simplest decisions. His secretary of eight years, Marlene, tried her best to protect him over the telephone and in his correspondence, but finally—with the frustration only an outstanding secretary can feel—said to him simply, "You've grown shortsighted," and he fired her.

Here she was, his right arm, a woman who adored him and her job, gathering her coat and purse. She said, "I'll be back for the plants," the way a wife at the end of her tether would say, "I'll be back for the children." She closed the door quietly on a ringing telephone.

It was worse with his kids. Gone from his vocabulary were affectionate terms of any kind, but especially "Short Stuff" for his son and "Little One" for his daughter. Now he growled around the house, pawing through cupboards for he-knew-not-what and prowling the yard in the wee hours with a desperate insomnia.

All of which drove—excuse me—a wedge between husband and wife. Loren didn't so much mind his tempers, as the children were old enough (ten and eleven) to know their father still loved them, and she didn't mind his rooting through the house for some unnamed—and unnameable—object, but she did mind missing him. Their fifteen-year marriage had always tipped deliciously between desire and gratification, but now he stalked around the neighborhood at night like a tomcat, and his absence from her bed was not something she could readily accept.

Patience was all well and good, but after a month of such behavior he bumped into the garbage cans out by the garage, and she rolled over to look at the clock. Two in the morning. She pushed up the window and stuck her head out.

"Ralph."

A now very quiet neighborhood listened back.

"Ralph! Ralph Fielding! Are you out there?"

"You'll wake the neighbors," he called up softly.

"Where are you?"

"In the shrubbery." And sure enough, Fielding stepped from the rhododendrons out into the driveway where she could see him.

"What the *hell* are you doing in the shrubbery?"

"Shh," he said.

She leaned farther over the casement and deliberately let herself spill out of her nightgown. "Can you see me, Ralph?"

"I can see you," he whispered.

"Well take a long look, buster."

"Loren—"

"If you tell me about the neighbors again," she said, "I'm going to lock you out of the house, too." And then, thinking that was a good idea in any case, she ran downstairs and did just that.

Fielding moved into a motel that night, a run-down place on the highway for twelve dollars a day, sixty-five for the week. *The Starlite.* This was a temporary obstruction, he knew. Loren would relent before the weekend, and he'd promise to behave better, and he'd apologize to the kids and take them to the zoo or to miniature golf, and everything would be fine. But as long as he had a couple of days to himself, and nights without fetters, he owed it to his game to get another set of clubs and put in some time at the range. By this time, though, he'd learned a truth about himself, so he bought clubs and cross-out balls at K-Mart.

He walked to the park that night with his new clubs under his arm like a bundle of firewood, and he carefully paced out fifty-nine yards. He split the grip of his new three iron with his pocket knife and peeled it off, then stabbed the club into the soil so it stood like a small metal flag. He paced fifty-nine yards back and dumped a dozen balls onto the grass. The sand wedge, first, he thought, determined that he would learn to hit each club—even the woods—close to the pin.

He got so good at ringing that makeshift flag that on the second night of practice he pulled off his shoes and set one in front of the three iron, and before morning he could drop a ball into it about one time in twenty. On the third night, standing barefooted, he'd aced his shoe with both wedges, the nine, the seven, and had bumped it with the four, five, and six. He broke his one recalcitrant club—the eight—over his knee, checked out of *The Starlite,* and went happily home.

"The bottoms of your feet are green," Loren said, as he sat on the edge of the bed, taking off his clothes.

"I know. I'm sorry," Fielding said, and waited patiently for her to invite him to bed.

"Get in," she said.

He got in.

He waited for Sunday, because Sunday is holy. He called ahead for a tee time, and he smiled and joked in the pro shop when he paid his greens fee. He waved jovially at the bartender through the windows, and the astonished bartender half raised a hand in return. He introduced himself to the threesome he'd been put with, and they all drove from the 1st tee.

Fielding birdied the hole and had the honor at the 2nd. "Pick a number between four and wedge," he told his partners.

"*Four?*" one of them asked.

"All right."

"No, I meant—"

"That's all right," Fielding said kindly. To everybody's amazement, he sat on the bench and removed his golf shoes and socks. He dropped his ball on the grass of the tee and took two practice putting strokes. "If it doesn't hit the pin," he said, "all the drinks are on me."

He got a Nicklaus look in his eye and swung.

●　●　●

"Give those louts whatever they want for as long as they want it," he told the bartender, "and give me a double whiskey. And so help me God if you talk to me you'll wish forever that you hadn't."

"I'll never forget it," one of them was telling the others. "No backswing to speak of, no follow-through, and that ball must've jumped two hundred yards and ended up near the 15th. I didn't know whether to shout *Fore!* or *Get a lawyer!*" He wiped his eye and drank. "But it was the prettiest damn four iron I've ever seen."

"Te*rrr*rific shot, lad," one of the others said in a gin-soaked, fake Scots burr, "save you're on the w*rrr*rong g*rrr*reen."

Hilarity on their part; an uncontrollable shaking in Fielding. The kid behind the bar sidled from sight and ran for the manager.

Fielding that night sat down to dinner with his family and asked each of them carefully how the day had gone. He appeared completely absorbed in each story—Will's bicycle adventures (street by street), Lorraine's backyard theatrical productions (scene by scene), Loren's bridge group (hand by hand)—and then after dinner he excused himself and said he'd better go and catch up on the work he'd let slide recently at the office.

He borrowed a pickup from a neighbor, drove to a twenty-four-hour rental shop, and put down good cash for a Rototiller.

"How long do you need it?" he was asked.

Fielding considered the driving time and the size of the green. "Have it back by midnight," he said with a calm he didn't feel.

No one life can take such strain. For three weeks, Fielding treated his new secretary with respect, his customers with thoughtfulness, and his family with devotion. His wife took him to parties, and he smiled. For three weeks, Fielding hardened inside and developed a cutproof cover, and not even

Loren suspected that something was terribly amiss. But tidal forces worked in him, and his shoreline began to erode.

"We have dinner next week up at the Hoffmans'," Loren said.

"I'd love another cup of coffee," he said.

Golf was the farthest subject from her mind, but suspicion, at the outset, is all-embracing. It bothered her, still, that he'd fired Marlene and wouldn't explain why. "Brunette or redhead in your coffee, dear?" she asked, being blonde.

"A little under sixty," he said.

"How little?"

"Fifty-nine yards."

Her immediate confusion quickly turned to concern. "Ralph? Are you all right?"

"I can't hit a four iron two hundred yards on a good day," he said with a bemused look. "Something's not right. Something large and horrible is at work here."

"Is this *golf*? But you've quit golf."

The children pushed their chairs back, preparing to flee.

"Gulp it? Of course I won't gulp it; it's hot, isn't it?"

"Scalding," she said, stricken.

"Top-Flite!"

She ran for the phone, and the doctor.

Given the episode at the start of the season, the doctor thought it best to hospitalize Fielding a second time.

"I'll look in on you tomorrow," the doctor said.

"I'm fine, thanks."

"Are you comfy?" the nurse asked.

"I'm fine, thanks."

"Ring the nurse if you need anything," the doctor said.

"I'm fine, thanks."

They closed the door softly and padded down the hall.

"I'm fine, thanks," Fielding said, and his roommate turned over in bed and drew the covers up over his face.

Though the fourth-floor staff girded themselves for violence, Fielding exhibited nothing but a continual puzzlement. He woke his roommate and himself more than once with a shout of "Fore!" or maybe "Four!" but neither Fielding nor his neighbor ever became aware of the nature of his nightmare.

He was released in a week with medicines that nobody had much confidence in.

The rest of Fielding's story is a downhill putt at Augusta.

He was a bankrupt before the end of the year. When the house was sold, Loren took the kids and went to live with her mother.

Fielding, shoeless now, and dressed in old clothes, took to hanging around under the trees near the 2nd at Cragmore. Sometimes he was given money, but mostly he was ignored. He wondered to himself (sometimes aloud) how everything could slip away so damned quickly, how a good life could become so irrevocably dismantled.

One clear, cold day late in the year he noticed another man among the trees near the 2nd tee, a man arrogantly dressed—but not for golf. It was Hallistone! but Fielding never knew that. The man made Fielding edgy in a way he couldn't articulate, and his hands itched once again to hold a club.

He darted from the trees and snatched an eight iron from a golfer's bag, took the ball from the stunned man's hand, and hit a soft shot that took two bounces and dived into the hole. Ace. Fielding raised his hands and danced. But the invaded foursome had been looking at Fielding and not at his shot, and the well-dressed gentleman smiled at Fielding with benign contempt. So what? his look said. Who couldn't ace it?

The golfer slid his club from Fielding's weak grip and hit the first of four shots within a gimme of the pin, and the foursome walked off with sidelong glances at each other and over-the-shoulder glances at Fielding, who stood empty-handed on the 2nd tee, a complete ruin.

CORPUS CHRISTI

Outside the window, the pink stucco back of a bowling alley blocked any view of the Gulf, but since Stevenson was more than a block from the beach there wouldn't have been much to see. There wasn't a breeze off the water; not a whiff of it, not even a suggestion of the salt smell that to a sailor means shore. The sky was a high, cloudless blue that bordered on white—such a dead heat that it sucked the color from everything, even the air, and made it invisible.

Inside the window, the room was hotter than the unmoving heat, with an invisibility of weight common to the Gulf coast of Texas or the swamplands of central Florida.

Stevenson stood at the window with his back to a suicide blonde named Trixie or Pixie or Roxie or something like that. Stevenson didn't care what she called herself anymore. He had cared the day before last, or perhaps the day before that, but for the last thirty hours he hadn't cared at all.

He was naked. He watched with bored interest as the sweat ran down his belly into the gray hair at his groin. If anyone were on the roof of the bowling alley, and for some reason facing away from the sea, and able to see through the glare that bounced off the windows like sheet lightning, Stevenson would simply have waved a hand and gone on standing there, striped by the blinds and boiled dry.

Trixie—it was Trixie, he decided—lay on the floor wearing only his boxer shorts. She was busy touching her knee to her nose. She'd been doing that for an hour like a senseless thing.

They had pulled the carpet up, and the pad, so she could lie on the stained cement underneath.

"Let's go to the beach," she said. "Stevie? Are you still breathing? Let's go to the beach."

Her voice, in this air, stayed even after the meaning was gone from her words. The room remained full of her voice—trapped in the corners like cockroaches. "The beach is too hot," he said. His voice dove out through the window, he was sure. "And it's not Stevie. It's not Mr. Stevenson. It's just Stevenson." He didn't bother to look back at her, although any other man would have. "The beach is too hot. Even the water's hot. Fill the tub up again."

"The water's brown."

"Is it cold?" Now Stevenson turned.

"No." She pouted and held her knee to her nose, so he had a pretty view of her packed youthful breasts and of her. He shrugged.

"What do you see out that window?" she asked.

He didn't say anything; when he brought her here with him on this business trip he'd known there wouldn't be anything to say. He hadn't cared then.

"How come everybody talks funny down here?"

He didn't answer.

"You think I've got a good figure?"

He heard the pout creeping back into her voice, and if he could placate her without using too much energy, he decided he would. He took a long look at her nakedness and managed to work his mouth into a grin. "What's not to like?" he said.

She stretched both legs out in front of her and pointed her toes, then sat up straight at the waist, a perfect right angle, sure of herself. "I guess," she said.

Stevenson started to turn back to the window.

"Come here," she said, dropping her voice into the low tone that had excited him once.

"Too beat," he said, and looked back at the bowling alley.

"I'm going shopping." She made it sound like a threat, though he couldn't imagine what kind of threat it could be.

"Better put something on first."

She didn't move from the rigid shape she'd got herself into. Stevenson saw now that he could see her reflection in the window and studied that.

Then he looked beyond it. Dirty white buildings rose up on each side of the bowling alley—both with ugly square windows and tipped at just the right angle to focus all their light and heat into his room. The heat was pulled up out of the water and sucked off all the shore of Texas and deflected off those two buildings into the second floor front he had rented for the week. Two floors higher and to the right he caught a flicker of movement. He stared until there was only that other window in his vision, and then only the horizontal bars of old venetian blinds, and then his eye seemed to travel between the dirty spaces until it was in the room. A form stood behind the shades, standing in the window as he was, waiting for a wind. He looked for a curve of hip or breast that would make it female, but didn't find one. He was suddenly sure that there were men standing in all the windows, just out of the reach of the light, all staring in the direction of the sea, waiting for a breath of wind to cool them.

Hundreds of men, he thought, all over Corpus Christi; thousands of them behind windows while thousands of women were scattered like used matchbooks, or flung out, a page at a time, like the morning paper on floors of apartments all across Texas.

He looked at the left-hand building and saw shapes in every window.

"Stevie?"

Sweat trickled down the crevice of his butt. "Yes?"

"How much longer?"

"How much longer, what?"

"What do you think, what?"

"How much longer in this room?" he asked. "Or how much longer in this town? Or how much longer until dinner? Or until we go to the beach, or go shopping, or how much longer until dark, or what?"

"Jesus, you're getting crabby." It was the pout again. The professional, feminine edge that slices words in half and leaves both sides bleeding. Women are born with it, he was convinced. Girl infants began learning it with their first breaths. He was convinced of this.

"It's hot," he said.

"How much longer"—she drew the word out and left a space after it—"until you hold me again?"

"Aren't you worn out?"

"No," she said. "Are you?"

"Yes. You've eviscerated me."

"What's *eviscerated*?"

He didn't really want to be unkind to her. "It means worn out," he said. "Almost. I'm not twenty anymore, though I wish I were, sometimes." He turned and looked at her, and made sure she knew he was looking. "I don't keep my back to you by accident."

She giggled. He faced the window again. Everything would be all right for a while longer. It bothered him that he could turn her this way and that without any effort.

"Stevie?"

"Huh."

"Let's take a shower."

"Hmm."

"Come on. A long shower."

"Oh."

"Only don't let my hair get wet."

"Why not?"

"The water's brown; I told you."

"You did."

She went in and turned the water on; he could hear the change of its sound as she stood under it and waited for him. He stayed at the window and ran a hand over his chest and pinched the slackness at his hips. "These were once steel," he said. "It used to be she'd have to bar the door." He was still there when she got tired of waiting and came back into the room, dripping over the rolled carpet, from the sound of it.

"Stevie?"

"Huh."

"I'm going to go crazy in this room."

"All right," he said, and left the window. "Put something on."

She tied a bikini on and then slipped under something that looked like a gauze curtain. She strapped rope sandals onto her feet. Stevenson pulled on a pair of white tennis shorts and let an unbuttoned yellow shirt hang from his shoulders.

"Are we going to the beach?"

"If you want."

She took one of the hotel towels off the rack. "Want one?"

He shook his head. They stepped into the hall. It was hotter out there than in the room.

"I forgot my sunglasses," she said. He unlocked the door for her and she went back. For a moment he thought about running—dodging down the stairs and taking the first two rights and the first left he came to, leaving her behind like you would a little sister. But she came out with a pair of red sunglasses while he was still thinking about it.

"Ready?" he asked.

She smiled and nodded. She really had an extraordinary smile.

The beach was too hot, and they didn't stay long. The heat came up from the sand through their shoes like molten metal. There were a hundred heads in the water, bobbing about like plastic cups. There was no one at all on the beach.

"Let's go somewhere air-conditioned," she said.

"We'd have to buy something."

"Okay."

He took her to a bar. They had two drinks each. The air conditioner rattled and wheezed and blew warm air, and he became annoyed at the steady hot draft in his face; it seemed to be setting his bones against each other.

"Let's go," he said, and she didn't argue.

They went back up to the room and peeled off their clothes. She sat down on the cement and he stood again at the window.

"That killed an hour," she said.

He only nodded. He was staring at the pink wall of the bowling alley and praying for rain. He asked God to give them a breeze. Even a little one. He shook his head to clear it.

"Something the matter?" she asked.

Stevenson shook his head to indicate no.

"Getting dizzy again?"

"I will if I have to keep shaking my head."

The heat had hit him the first day and blurred his vision. He'd had to lie down as soon as they got into the room, and it was all right, then, that she had joined him. But now they had two days to go, and he thought maybe he couldn't last—that he'd have to cancel his appointments and catch a flight home. The heat now seemed his business here, and he had lost.

Something tugged at his inner ear. "What?" he asked.

"I didn't say anything."

"Are you sure?"

"Sure I'm sure."

Maybe it was her voice, stirring in the room from some dead sentence. It tugged again, and he realized it was an outside sound, far off. "Hear that?"

"I don't hear anything."

"It was a rumble." He stretched up on his toes, as if he could see over the bowling alley with another inch of height.

"Probably an airplane," she said.

He shook his head.

"Or a truck."

He shook it again.

"Or a bus." She would go down the entire list, he knew.

"Listen," he said. "Shh."

In another minute, he heard it again.

"Thunder," he said.

She joined him at the window. He was aware of her breast against his biceps, and the hairs on his leg stood up, warning him of her.

"You really think so?"

It happened again, and they both heard it. The sky to the east looked like old copper.

"See that?" he asked. "Does that sky look green?"

"It sure does."

While they were watching it, it flickered, as if it had been shaken.

"Lightning," he said. "It's going to rain."

The street darkened and a squall swept across the water and over them with frightening speed, even though it promised what he wanted, and spattered the window with running streaks. The bowling alley lost its pink and turned a muddy color.

"Roof," he said, and pulled on his shorts. "Put something on."

He ran out and started up the steps without waiting for her to follow. He heard the door shut and then her feet on the hot metal stairway. He ran up three flights and pushed open the door to the roof. It was flat, white, empty; heat came up from it in curtains.

She pushed out behind him and tugged on the waistband of his shorts. The sky was dark green and glittered with gold inside.

"Is it safe up here?" she asked.

"Who cares?"

The rain came in a wall that sent him backward a few steps and bounced off the roof like hail. If she hadn't had a good grip on his shorts she would have gone down.

She let out a whoop and let go of his shorts and started dancing, flinging her feet up until they touched her hands with an unjointed ease that astonished him. He lifted up his hands and whooped along with her.

She had put on that gauzy shirt again, but without the bikini underneath. The rain plastered it to her skin until it looked like she was wearing cellophane—or not even that, but transparent skin like a reptile's that needed shedding. She didn't look wet. She was dark brown at the nipples and groin, and pink everywhere else, and she seemed to light up from the inside as her skin drew in the water. From him it rolled off in rivers and waterfalls, but she absorbed it all and glowed.

He walked over and slowly pulled the gauze wrapper off, up

over her wet skin and outstretched arms, and she brought
her arms down around his neck and kissed him. Ah, peace,
he thought, and hoisted her up to his waist and tried to hold
on and keep his legs from shaking as they made love upright
under the green sky and lightning, and then he saw through
her to the window where he stood looking out, and felt that
the form or the figure across the way had turned and was
looking down into him.

PULL, PONIES, PULL, MY DEARHEARTS

He is the last of us, or if not the last, the next to last, or the next to that. Most of a decade has gone since he's seen another like himself, so whatever the number it's slim enough to hold in the left hand and still haw the horses. *Get around, there. Glide, I said. Sideways, you. Pull, you long-haired piebalds.* That hand is curled like a horseshoe from being stepped on.

Crouching over the high seat worn smooth by his bottom, swaying because a team has eight legs and he has only two, he half-stands like Adam and calls their names. *Pull, skewbalds.* They'd pull, probably, even if he didn't call out to them *(Hey! Pull, darlin's),* but words tumble from him like breath itself, and always have. They form like clouds in the clear air under his long nose.

He kicks at the bucket hanging from the brake. Their ears flick forward, and together—the three of them—they pull into a trot.

Downhill, now, ladies. You lovelies. A mile and a quarter away lies the next town—*Kallisburne, the sign says*—and trouble, like always.

Kallisburne was a village before people knew they wanted such a thing. It collected itself, like gravity, around an upright, tapered stone.

Fires were lit, and then relit, and then not let to go out. As long as wood was being carried to it in any case, trees were soon hewn and walls raised, and in time those walls became an inn. It grew upwards. Underneath, where the men like to drink, the dirt of its basement floor is blue, but not clay, and hard-packed by generations of patient standing into something as good as rock, and the central pillar that keeps the floor above from dropping on them is that monolith three times the height of a man. The base of it is buried beyond any further digging.

Kallisburne is his destination because it's in his way and it has an inn that sells whiskey, and not because that inn has a stone driven into its floor like a wedge. He kicks the bucket twice with his metal-toed boot and sings to his horses:

> *I'll eat when I'm hungry, I'll drink when I'm dry,*
> *An' if whiskey don't kill me I'll live till I die.*

Ha! now. Hop! Hop!

It's midday when he sets the brake in front of the inn and lets the reins pool at his feet. A clowder of dogs comes from nowhere. They arrange themselves in a circle about his wagon, taking their places as if they'd picked them out beforehand. He thinks how strange, how feline they look, standing with bowed backs, watching. His right-hand horse shakes her neck in her hame and bells jingle. A door or a shutter closes somewhere down the street, but except for that and the ringing still in his inner ear, it is quiet.

"Well, now," he says in the language he uses around people. "Go and fetch your masters."

He lights a pipe while he's waiting, cupping the match in his bent hand. When the ironclad door of the inn is opened and the men file out, the whiskey smell roils into the street in a mist. His head and the horses' come up as one to breathe it in.

"Good day to you," he says, and blows a cloud at them.

"You've come for a drink," one of them says.

"If that's an invitation, I'll do just that." He nods, as if to himself. "That sounds fine."

"What brings you here?" another asks. "Are you one of those tinkers?"

"I can be," he says. "I can be whatever you need. Just now I'm only thirsty."

He hears someone mutter, "Gypsy."

"Once," he says, and grins at all of them. Then he shakes his head. "Not anymore."

He steps down from his high seat and they make a path for him, reluctantly, pushing the dogs away with their boots. He nods his thanks and goes into the inn.

"This way, then," one of the men says, his hospitality warring with his hatred, and leads the way into the cellar.

He brushes against the cold stone. His fingertips rest for a moment against it, and it almost stops him on his way to the heavy plank that is the bar. "Whiskey," he says, and lets a coin fall from his palm. When he has it, he turns to face them and lifts the glass in a toast. "Life."

He knocks it back. He likes the way it races into his empty stomach. "Once again."

The men arrange themselves around him in a half-circle, the way the dogs in the street had, silent, watching.

"Ran the last Gypsy out a dozen or more years ago," one of them finally says. "After he thieved a sheep."

"Did you, now? Did you run a poor old man out into the wild because he was hungry? The all of you on one side, and him on the other? Is that the sort of town I'm in?"

"It is."

"Those dogs of yours don't need voices," he says, and drinks his second whiskey.

"Meanin'?"

"Meanin' there's growls enough in you." Without turning his back on them, he says, "Once again, if I've change left over."

After a minute, one of them nods an answer to the barman's silent question, and he hears the heavy shot glass strike the plank behind him.

"Ah, now, that's fine." But he doesn't reach for it. He doesn't know how he can without dislocating a shoulder.

"Go ahead and drink it, old man. Drink all you'll have and then go."

"Drink all I'll have? You haven't enough."

"Drink all you can pay for, then," that same man says, and forces his lips into a smile.

"You've still not enough."

"Haven't we? Where's your gold, then? In your pockets or your wagon?"

He puts on a sly look. "You sure you didn't thieve that sheep from the Romany, and not the other way around?"

"Here, now."

"Are you lookin' to steal my horses?" He smiles widely, knowing the gold in his front tooth will be winking. "Help! Help!" He turns and picks up the shot with two fingers of his good right hand and sends the whiskey in it skidding down his throat. "Once again, if you please."

"Your change has run out," the barman says.

He lets another coin drop. Gets his whiskey. With his back still to them, he drinks it down in a swallow like the others. "How much for the bottle?"

"Give it to him," a voice behind him says. "And you might think of taking it with you."

He turns. "That's the rub of it, eh? That I might think of taking it with me? What is it you have that you're so afraid I'll be stealing?" His eyes move across their faces and leave marks. "Your women? Your livestock?" He takes in the stone. "That?"

"All the thievin' sons of your kind together couldn't budge that stone."

"I could move it," he says, "if I wanted." He takes the bottle from the barman's hand and goes over unsteadily to investigate. "A man raised it up, once; a man can take it back down."

"*A* man, he says. A *civilization,* he means. He can't hold his drink."

"You think these great stones all over the world get up by their ownselves? You think men work together for generations to do it? Don't you know when you give four men a job to do that in an hour two of them will be watching?" He runs his hand along its surface and feels the cold centuries stored inside it. "No, gentlemen. A man like me raised this stone by himself." He looks into their faces. "It was a mistake, of course."

"A mistake, is it?"

"Aye." He nods, no longer thinking of them and their poor lives, but of his own, and is genuinely sad. "It's the travelin' people put up these stones. Here, and in England and in America, and in the deserts and the jungles all over the round globe. This beauty"—he taps it—"is part of a large circle you can't see, and those circles part of a larger one, like the workings of an engine." He shrugs. "It's a mathematics we've lost."

"Too heavy for any one man," one says.

"He's a mathemagician now," says another.

"Too heavy for a man without mathematics," he agrees. He almost tells them what he knows: *that it's freemasonry and transcendental numbers and knowing the balancing point of fields,* but he doesn't; he takes a drink from the bottle instead.

And then undoes his best intentions. "The stones are in circles, like I said. Used to be they were raised in pairs and crossed by another, a lintel. The old Greeks, now, when they found them, they used that for their fourth letter, that's *pi,* which is the ratio of the circumference of a circle to its diameter, which means it's three times longer to go around something than to cut straight across it.

"And then in other places, there's pyramids—four-sided triangles—and many more of them than you might think. That's the sixteenth letter, *delta,* which is the way those same old Greeks determined variation in increments a man can understand. Four-times-four, do you see?"

He shakes his head at them, having only a glimmer of the pattern himself: that the circle is space, the pyramid is time. "But pi is infinitely variable; it goes on without repeating itself. Why am I askin' you if you can see it? You're farmers and the like, drawn to the magic of a stone put up to mark your way."

"He's drunk already."

Which reminds him he is holding a bottle. He tips it up and swallows until tears start. "Yes, I am," he says, when he's got his breath. "Or getting damned near it, at least.

"You're not supposed to be livin' out your lives at a stone. It's a marker, a milestone, no more than that. It's here for you to set up camp around, but not *forever*." He sighs. "Not forever. You've got to travel the whole circuit."

"Then what?"

"That takes all the time a man has," he says. "And maybe some more besides."

"I'll be damned to stand here and listen to a madman," one of them says, and goes up the stairs.

"If a man's lost the whole truth, then he's mad," he calls after him. "An' you're right! I have. And so I am." He takes another long pull on the bottle. "But what do you call a man that hasn't got any notion of it to start with? I have enough of it left in me to know to keep movin', which is more than you've got, and I know, too, sad to say, that the likes of you and all mankind won't allow it anymore." He lays his hand on the stone. "This stone's more mine than yours and it's a pity we ever put it up. It's come to mean everything it shouldn't."

He's got the hiccoughs, now. "Soon, all of us with any—imagination whatsoever will be—gone, and see what that gets the rest of you. Dam—nation."

"Take that bottle with you," one of them says.

"You're not wanted here," says another.

"Do tell? La-de-da." He waves the bottle in a circle and lifts his bad hand as if to bless them. But it looks too much like a scythe, even to him. "Ah—hell," he says, and belches, and goes up.

He's got a team that can pull him without any of his help, so he kicks at the bucket to get them started and they rock him to sleep on his high seat. He goes down into it without fighting.

The horses come to a fork and stop, as they're used to doing. They smell water the lower way, where the road goes down to a creek, so when instructions aren't forthcoming they take that path and when they come to the creek they wade in and drink. They're still standing there when it grows dark.

He opens his eyes to the first few stars and his nostrils to the weedy smell of gentle water. His left-hand horse is blowing noisily, wanting to go. *Hah!* he tells her. *Pull, then.*

He leans down and drags the bucket through it. The wagon bumps across the creek bottom and up the other bank, and he reins them to another stop under some trees. *You'll be wantin' out of those corsets, girls,* he tells them. *An' one of these days I'll be showing you how to do it for yourselves.*

When he has his pair hobbled to graze and a fire and a poor stew begun, he's wide awake with hunger and a whiskey-thirst. The anger he'd gone to sleep with is awake again, too.

"Fools," he calls back in the town's direction. "Rooted as rocks, all of you."

He must have dropped the bottle, or finished it. Perhaps he drank it while he was sleeping. Now there's a waste, he says to himself. I hate when I do that.

It's nights like this one that he wants company. Not the female kind, and not his ponies, but a man his own age and experience he can argue with, take a swing at, share a bottle with, and then sing bawdy harmony as the dawn springs up around them. One a baritone, one a tenor, waking the forest creatures. It's nights like this one that he remembers whole tribes of others like himself meeting at a crossroads or a field, and one of those standing stones somewhere in sight. Remembers helping his brothers borrow a head or two of cattle and then watching them kneel under his father's hammer, and then keeping the fire. Remembers passing the whiskey from one man to another, the warm glass bottle in his palm for only a part of a minute. It's nights like this one that he's most aware that an age has passed since this life was full and round.

Out of his maudlin sadness, his anger boils up again. Ridicule him, will they? Accuse him for a thief and run him out before he's had his fill? What was it the one had called him? *A mathemagician.*

His ponies snort and paw the ground. *Easy, there. Don't be catchin' my mood, lovelies. Get your rest, darlin's.*

He looks at the stars and figures the time, figures it back to passing out, and, knowing the rate his team walks, finds the difference. What he doesn't know is how long they stood in the creek. Most of an afternoon, he decides. They're pigs for water. He banks the fire.

In no more than an hour he knows he's right; Kallisburne is only a stretch of the legs from where he's camped. It's not a large enough place that it can be said with any honesty to spread out before him, but there it is, anyway: a loose collection of homes gathered—huddled, rather—around the inn as if no harm can ever come. As if that stone will save it.

He looks at its layout with an engineer's eye. With a good northeast wind, one thoughtful torch might do the whole job for him. But there's no breeze at all tonight. And he might wait a year before he'd feel one from that compass point. No, he'll not wreck this town with flame.

He walks in the middle of the road, whistling like a child. He goes into the inn and down the stairs. He pushes through the dozen men there and puts his good, flat palm against the plank and politely asks for a whiskey.

The fear in their eyes is enough. Almost.

"You'll be owin' me for that last bottle, then," the barman says.

He shrugs and carefully stacks half a dozen coins on the bar. When he has his whiskey—a bit short, to his thinking— he raises it to all. "Health," he says, and then he doesn't drink it.

Hands flick to their faces to ward off evil.

He's amused at that. "Too late," he says, "by several centuries," and then he takes the whiskey the way he takes a breath. "Ah. Well, now, let's have a look at this stone of yours while the good barman pours me another."

He might be a doctor of monoliths, the way he lays his hands on it, rubbing and probing and um-humming. He is a gynecologist of stones. He strokes one smooth, nearly blue flank. He reaches behind on each side so it appears he's hugging it, and then with his head flat against one wall he peers into the place it joins the plaster. There's gaps.

He takes a long, great, slow pleasure in violating their stone. He sees that they are nervous, and sees that they are uncomfortable admitting even to themselves the reasons for their concern, and sees, too, that his bravado has them confused. He carries small hammers in his wagon for working tin, but not the sledge he needs for this.

"Well," he says, and strokes his chin and reaches absently for his drink. "It's a good enough stone, I suppose."

"Here, now. You stop foolin' with it."

"What are you afraid of, man?" he asks slowly. "What are you afraid of, any of you? *That I might tumble this thing like I promised? What would your lives be like, then, I wonder?* Could you farm your lands without that stone still upright in this cellar? Could you raise your children? Love your wives? Could aught that you are be rooted here with this?" He hefts his shot glass like a small rock and then lobs it gently at the monolith. "Are you too afraid to find out?"

His words, and the glass shattering against the stone, and their inarticulate cries of frustrated rage, and their rough, hard, square hands on his shoulders are all caught up for him in the same frozen moment, and always will be.

He goes down under them like grass under a boot, bent parallel, his shoes still miraculously sticking to the floor for an instant before he's flat on that hard earth. He's able to land one awkward upright punch and kick one shin before he's thudded insensible.

•   •   •

They've left him at the edge of the village in a ditch the rain has cut. He breathes, and cries out. A rib, at the least, is broken. His left hand twists back on itself so the curled, upward-looking palm stares at him like a dry socket. He gets up shakily, hoping his legs work, and when he finds they do, he starts off for his camp.

He is beyond rage, now, and will gladly give all he owns to have his revenge. *Here, dearhearts. Come to me, ponies. That's right; that's right.*

He strokes their noses, hooking a finger into one nostril and petting the inside. One of them nuzzles his armpit and he jumps back and cries out again.

The rope he has in the wagon is in use. He has to unlash his belongings and splice two ends together—all of this one-and-a-half-handed and with his teeth—and then coil the long length around his middle. His camp is a litter now of all he owns, of every place he's been. He yokes the ponies together and, riding one, drives them into the village.

This time when they see him they run to their barns for pitchforks and long-helved tools, or to their homes for guns. But even drawing painful breaths as he is, he has limped into the inn and back out again before they reach him, the rope wrapped around that upright stone and secured to the horse collars.

He whips the right-hand horse with the rope's bitter end. *Ha! Pull, ponies. Pull, my dearhearts.*

As the villagers race toward him silently in the midst of their dogs, he swears he feels the stone give, but it is the hames and harness slipping from underneath him.

Acknowledgments

I am grateful to the Pennsylvania Council on the Arts for a grant that has helped support my fiction.

I am grateful, too, to Melanie J. Harris for preparing this manuscript and for helping me coax another couple thousand pages of my fiction into the electronic age.

I am grateful most of all to Gloria Thomas, whose editorial suggestions made these stories better.

Three of these stories first appeared in substantially the same form in the following publications: "Corpus Christi" in *GQ* in 1986; "Always Cold" in *Missouri Review* in 1992; and "Playing Out of the Deep Woods" in *New Myths/MSS* in 1994. I thank Trish Deitch Rohrer, Greg Michalson, and Bob Mooney, respectively.

ABOUT THE AUTHOR

Courtesy of Lycoming College

G. W. Hawkes is the author of *Spies in the Blue Smoke* (University of Missouri Press). His stories have appeared in a wide variety of distinguished magazines, including *GQ* and *Atlantic Monthly*. He teaches English at Lycoming College in Williamsport, Pennsylvania.